the death code

(a remi laurent fbi suspense thriller—book 1)

ava strong

Ava Strong

Debut author Ava Strong is author of the REMI LAURENT mystery series, comprising three books (and counting); of the ILSE BECK mystery series, comprising four books (and counting); and of the STELLA FALL psychological suspense thriller series, comprising three books (and counting).

An avid reader and lifelong fan of the mystery and thriller genres, Ava loves to hear from you, so please feel free to visit www.avastrongauthor.com to learn more and stay in touch.

ISBN: 978-1-0943-9283-7

BOOKS BY AVA STRONG

REMI LAURENT FBI SUSPENSE THRILLER
THE DEATH CODE (Book #1)
THE MURDER CODE (Book #2)
THE MALICE CODE (Book #3)

ILSE BECK FBI SUSPENSE THRILLER
NOT LIKE US (Book #1)
NOT LIKE HE SEEMED (Book #2)
NOT LIKE YESTERDAY (Book #3)
NOT LIKE THIS (Book #4)

STELLA FALL PSYCHOLOGICAL SUSPENSE THRILLER
HIS OTHER WIFE (Book #1)
HIS OTHER LIE (Book #2)
HIS OTHER SECRET (Book #3)

PROLOGUE

Glencairn Museum, Bryn Athyn, Pennsylvania
Midnight

Ted Peterson walked through the Great Hall, his shoes echoing in the darkness as he moved the beam of his flashlight around. Twenty years on the job next month and he still couldn't get over the beauty of this place.

The Great Hall was built to resemble some palatial feasting room of medieval Europe. Ted's light played over a couple of saint statues and some centuries-old furniture of velvet and mahogany before moving up to the balcony where, along the wall, hung several different types of polearms. Ted knew the names of them all. Halberd. Glaive. Spetum. His light reached toward the ceiling, the darkness of the vast space swallowing the beam to allow only the shadowy hint of Gothic arches and wooden beams.

His light moved down, running along the keen edge of a German Zweihander sword nearly as long as his own 5'8" height before moving to the graceful tripartite stained-glass windows.

Ted stopped before reaching them and let out a sigh. During the day, with the light streaming through, the saints on them glowed with breathtaking color and the floor of the great hall was carpeted in a rainbow pattern.

He played his light over the figures, catching a faint glimmer of the light he knew he'd see in tomorrow's glorious sunrise, and smiled. He always made sure to be in the Great Hall at sunrise.

The security guard headed out of the Great Hall, continuing his rounds. He paused at an Ottonian ivory in its glass case. It was the cover of some book from the 10th century, the volume itself long vanished, leaving only its glorious cover. A delicately carved crucifixion was framed with a border of colorful enamel and gold filigree, a masterpiece of pre-Renaissance art. The beam of his flashlight made the centuries-old ivory seem almost translucent and gleamed off the colored enamel and gold.

And they called this era the Dark Ages?

Ted smiled. Of the more than 8,000 objects in the museum, this was one of his favorites. Such detail! So much work and artistry had gone into it!

He could give an hour-long lecture on just this piece. In fact, he could do the same with most of the objects here thanks to the years of enthusiastic reading and a few precious trips he'd managed to pay for by scrimping and saving from his meager salary.

Yeah, this job paid pretty badly. At least he didn't have a wife or kids to support. And at least his spirit, and his eyes, were rich.

How couldn't they be in this place?

If only they made him a docent. He was more than qualified, except for the fact that he only had a high school education. The board of directors only cared about the piece of paper, not the person behind it.

And, truth be told, he'd never been good with people. He never could think of what to say, and when he did say something, it came out all wrong. Ted Peterson felt more at home in museums than bars, more comfortable reading than socializing. He doubted he could hold an audience, even an interested one.

He'd never be anything more than a watchman.

Ted sighed. Oh, well. At least he got to work in a place of beauty and history.

A distant crash made him turn, heart skipping a beat. It sounded like it came from the east stairway. He hurried that way, adrenaline pumping. In all his years here, he'd only had to deal with intruders once, when some kids from the local high school had broken in on a dare. They'd been so scared when he caught them that he'd spent most of the ten minutes it took the police to arrive trying to calm them down.

Could it be more kids? Or maybe a real burglar this time? He felt fear, but also a protectiveness. If it was a burglar, the guy would have to reckon with Ted Peterson.

Heart beating fast, he passed through the Italian Renaissance room, his light zigzagging across delicate paintings of the Virgin Mary and elaborate bronzes of Classical themes until he came to the staircase.

And stopped.

No one was in sight.

But at the head of the stairs stood a pedestal that usually held a plaster bust of the great historian Edward Gibbon. Now the bust lay on the marble floor, shattered into a dozen pieces.

Ted stood listening for a moment. Not a sound.

Shining his flashlight all around and seeing no one, he tiptoed to the broken bust. Something looked strange about it.

He leaned closer, blinking with confusion. The bust was hollow. He could see from a portion of the top of the head and a big chunk of one side that there had been a space inside, about the size of a paperback.

"Took you long enough."

The soft whisper coming from the Italian Renaissance Room shoved his heart up to his throat and made him spin around.

He took a couple of hesitant steps forward and shone his flashlight all around the room he had just passed through. No one, and no place to hide. There hadn't been anyone when he went through just a few seconds ago, and there wasn't anyone here now.

But the voice had come from here.

There was something else strange about that voice. It had sounded like a child, a young boy.

A soft step behind him.

Before he could turn, a strong arm pinioned both his own to his sides, and he felt the cold, keen edge of a knife set against his throat.

"Sounds can be deceiving," a hoarse voice rasped in his ear.

Ted trembled, more from the voice than the strong arm or even the knife. He heard madness in that voice.

"P-please," Ted stammered. "I didn't see your face. I can't identify you."

"No one ever does."

"Just go. Please. I got a family."

Actually, he didn't. No wife. No kids. A sister in another state he barely talked to. Hardly any friends even. He'd always been a bit of a recluse. That was why he volunteered for the night shift. To be alone. Comfortable. But maybe that had been a mistake. Maybe he should have tried harder. Reached out more.

"Thy will be done," the voice intoned in a rough croak.

Ted Peterson felt the knife cut into his throat in a cold slice of pain. Hot blood burst out of the gaping wound. He choked on it, gasping for breath that wouldn't come. His desperate inhalation made a sickly sucking sound through the gap in his throat. His lungs filled with blood. Ted was drowning.

His legs gave out. The man let him go, and Ted fell to the floor. The only things he felt now were pain and regret.

The second-to-last thing Ted Peterson saw in the light of his flashlight as it fell beside him was a pair of black boots caked with bright red mud. What was that sparkling in the mud stain? Something bright, like flecks of gold.

Then his weakened eyes lowered, and the last thing he saw was the expanding pool of his own blood.

CHAPTER ONE

Quantico, Virginia
The next morning

Agent Daniel Walker hurried up the steps of the FBI Headquarters administration building, ignoring the beautiful spring day and the greeting of a colleague going down. He was in trouble again; he just knew it. Roughing up that witness had been a bad idea.

But how the hell was he going to catch the Finger Man if people didn't cooperate?

And hey, the guy was a ketamine dealer. He deserved a good toileting anyway.

Walker was being brought up for review. It was the only explanation for being called to a surprise meeting with the deputy director.

And to make matters worse, he was late.

Checking his watch, he went through the metal detector and checked in with the security officer at the front desk. Seeing a line in front of the elevator, he took the stairs three at a time up four stories to the deputy director's office. He stopped long enough in the corridor to straighten his tie and flap his suit to cool himself off a bit. He really shouldn't be so out of breath. He was only 40, but a taste for beer and fast food and a distaste for the gym, had begun to catch up with him.

Squaring his shoulders, he passed through the door marked "Deputy Director Burton."

"You're late, of course," the deputy director's personal assistant said. Flora Whitaker was a cool, professional woman approaching retirement age who had seen many administrations come and go. She had a droopy face, wore far too much makeup, and yet had a sharp gaze that took in everything. Invulnerable in her position, she had a habit of saying all the things other people were too polite or too politic to say.

"Sorry, got a new lead in the case."

To Daniel, Deputy Director Burton's front office, with its Ficus plant, photo of the president, and glaring personal assistant behind an expansive desk felt like the River Styx. And Flora Whitaker was Charon.

She narrowed her eyes in her classic "don't try that on me" expression that had broken many an agent and nodded toward the door to a meeting room. "Pass on through. They've probably fallen asleep by now."

They?

Glancing at the door to Burton's office and wondering why he wasn't going in there as he expected, he went over to the meeting room door, knocked, and was called to enter.

He opened the door and froze.

Deputy Director Burton sat at the head of a long black table, a couple of file folders lying in front of him. He was an erect, rugged man in his seventies who still retained the buzzcut he first sported in Vietnam. Flanking him were the hunched and paunchy Personnel Director, Daniel Walker's direct boss, the Assistant Director for the Behavioral Analysis Unit who looked like a younger version of Burton, and … somebody else.

I didn't drown the creep, did I?

The somebody else, an attractive woman in her forties who looked Japanese but spoke with a rather jarring Texas drawl, said, "Agent Walker, how kind of you to join us. Do please sit down."

Crap. She's probably not even FBI. She's probably a lawyer or something bringing me up on assault charges. And the personnel director? He's here to fire me.

Daniel sat warily at the end of the table, looking across a good ten feet of unoccupied space at the important figures clustered at the other end. This setup was what the psychologists called a "nonverbal cue of dominance." He called it the prelude to the mother of all chewings out.

Deputy Director Burton gestured to the Japanese American woman. "This is Keiko Ochiai, Assistant Director of the Antiquities Division."

Daniel nodded at the woman, confused. "Pleased to meet you, Professor Ochiai. Which university to you teach at?"

The woman smiled. "I'm not a professor, I'm an agent with the FBI just like you. I can understand your confusion. The Antiquities Division is a new branch of the FBI, established just last week."

"Oh."

"The Bureau decided to open the Antiquities Department due to a sharp rise in illegal antiquities smuggling. As I'm sure you are aware, many terror groups such as ISIS and Al Qaeda loot archaeological sites and sell the objects they find on the illegal antiquities market. They use the money to buy arms. While many other agencies already cover this area, the Bureau felt it would be good to have its own department because there wasn't enough of a national focus on this problem. It's seen as an international issue, but many of the buyers and dealers are right here in the United States. Sadly, so are some of the terror cells."

"Sounds like it's needed," Daniel said, still unclear on where she was going with this. "I wish you the best of luck."

Assistant Director Ochiai smiled. "I won't need luck with a qualified agent such as you to help."

Daniel blinked. "I don't follow."

Deputy Director Burton slid a file folder down the length of the table. It was one of his favorite tricks. The table was smooth, freshly waxed every morning, and he did not allow it to be cluttered with pitchers of water and coffee mugs like in so many other meeting rooms. Only work-related materials were allowed on his table. This gave him more room to slide documents.

The folder whooshed unerringly to Daniel's waiting hands. A paperclip held it shut. Burton's little trick wouldn't be so impressive if the folder flew open and papers launched out like confetti.

Anytime Burton slid a folder down the table at a meeting, which was every meeting, Daniel felt like shouting "INCOMING!!!" to see if the deputy director would have a Nam flashback.

He had never dared. Despite being thirty years older, Burton could probably kick his ass.

"A night watchman at the Glencairn Museum in Pennsylvania was murdered last night by an unknown intruder," the deputy director said. "Although one object was broken, nothing was stolen."

Daniel opened the folder to see a photo of an employee tag for someone named Ted Peterson. The photo showed a smiling, nondescript man in his late forties or early fifties.

"The intruder was a pro," Burton went on. "Disabled a sophisticated alarm system and picked the lock on the service entrance. Once inside, he disabled the security cameras. We think the night watchman caught him in the act or got alerted by the sound of a breaking plaster bust, which was the only object that was disturbed."

Daniel flipped through the pages, intrigued as he was any time he heard about a new case. Even the simplest murder always had some twist, some unusual element. There seemed to be no limit to how human drama could lead to deadly consequences.

He thumbed through several stills from the security footage, enlarged and digitally enhanced. They were in sequential order and showed a masked man in heavy boots and dressed all in black coming into view at the side of the building where a short flight of steps led down to the metal door of the service entrance. Some closeups showed him fiddling with the electronics of the alarm system before picking the lock. A final shot showed him just inside the service entrance working on the control box for the security cameras.

"Light-skinned male, strong build, six-foot-two, right-handed," Daniel said.

"A good eye as always, Agent Walker," Deputy Director Burton said.

Feeling more confident because of this compliment, Daniel flipped through more pages of the folder, mildly intrigued.

"Both the alarm and CCTV systems are top of the line," Daniel went on. "The time tags reveal that he disabled those and unlocked the door all in less than five minutes. Your man knows what he's doing."

"Your man, Agent Walker," the deputy director said.

Daniel looked up at him. "My man? I specialize in serial killers."

So I'm not *in trouble for putting a drug dealer's head in a toilet and flushing?*

"This might be one." Burton slid another folder down the table. Daniel stopped it, removed the paperclip, and examined the papers inside.

"The night before last, a security guard was killed at the Cloisters in New York City. It's a medieval religious building brought over from France."

"Actually, four different buildings," Daniel said absently as he looked through the papers, which included security camera stills and a report from the NYPD. Same M.O. from what looked like the same perp. He had disabled the alarm and cameras, picked the lock on a back door, and entered. The guard was found dead with his throat slit next to a broken ivory figurine.

Daniel absentmindedly tapped the table with his thumb. Interesting. A highly motivated, skilled killer who had very specific targets. Shouldn't be too hard to track down. Fascinating to interview, though.

He made a mental note to review the recording once Ochiai's team nabbed the guy.

"We think it's the same man," Ochiai said.

"It is," Daniel said with a nod. "But he isn't a serial killer. There's too much deliberation, and no trophy taking. It says here nothing was stolen and he didn't mutilate the bodies. Plus, serial killers usually go for the vulnerable. They don't like to break and enter secure buildings. That takes too much planning for their rollercoaster of emotions. And there doesn't appear to be any ritualistic aspect, not like Finger Man."

"Finger Man?" Assistant Director Ochiai asked.

"That's what my partner, Agent Nomellini, and I call the serial killer we're tracking. He murders athletic young blonde males on their way out of late-night gyms. He always removes the middle finger of the right hand. So we call him Finger Man."

Daniel studied the chief of the new Antiquities Division as he said all this, looking for a reaction. She showed no reaction at all.

Well, at least you've been around the block. Not like some of these pencil pushers. The personnel director looks like he's going to lose his morning bagel.

"Your partner will have to get on without you," Assistant Director Ochiai said. "From now on you'll be working under me, effective immediately."

"Wait. What? Finger Man has killed eight young men so far. We're just beginning to close in on him. If I leave the case now—"

"Agent Nomellini is perfectly capable," the deputy director said.

"She's one of the best in the business." *Second only to me,* Daniel added silently. "This is a highly complex case, though. Hundreds of strands of evidence. And the clock is ticking. He hasn't killed in a month. He's past due. If we don't get him pretty soon there's going to be a ninth victim."

"We're giving her Agent Dunning to help."

Dunning? He's out in the park half the time watching porn on his phone. If Nomellini finds out, she'll turn into Finger Woman.

Daniel managed not to say that. Barely. Instead, he said, "I'm more qualified than Dunning. Why don't you give him this case? This looks pretty straightforward. Obviously, the perp's got a grudge against museums for some reason. He doesn't have the traits of a serial killer. In fact, he might be finished already if all he wanted to do was strike back at these two museums. Finger Man won't stop until he's caught."

"We believe this to be the more complicated case," Ochiai said. "And one suited to your special abilities."

"I'm a profiler, not an antiquities expert."

"You have a B.A. in history from Tufts. You dropped out of graduate school to join the FBI. If you hadn't, judging from what your old professors say, you could have had tenure by now."

"I didn't want to be in academia."

Not after Lyons. Or Rome. Or Aachen.

Not after she believed him instead of me.

"Nevertheless, you have a knack for solving historical puzzles. I read about the Colonial Williamsburg case."

That old case? That was years ago. Damn, she does her homework.

"I solved that by profiling the killer and figuring out who among the staff fit the profile."

"That and an intimate knowledge of black powder firearms," Ochiai said with a smile.

Daniel shrugged. "A hobby of mine. I'm a bit old school. Hunting with a musket is a lot more challenging than hunting with a high-powered rifle fitted with a scope. Do you like venison?" he asked, hoping she was a vegetarian.

Assistant Director Ochiai grinned. "I prefer beef. I'm a Texas girl."

"You also won the FBI marksmanship award three years running," said Martin Bradshaw, the Assistant Director for the Behavioral Analysis Unit. His salt and pepper hair showed no sign of receding despite his being close to retirement age, but his craggy face was deeply seamed with worry lines.

"You beat me the fourth year," Daniel told his boss. "Pity we weren't using muskets."

Bradshaw chuckled. Daniel liked the guy. He understood how investigations really had to be conducted, not what the FBI code of conduct said. He had covered for Daniel several times.

But it didn't look like he was going to cover for him now.

Daniel addressed him directly, hoping his boss might throw him a lifeline. "Agent Nomellini and I are getting close. I can feel it. I really need to stay on this case."

To his dismay, Bradshaw shook his head. "You're much better placed in the Antiquities Division."

The Personnel Director cut in, still looking queasy. A pencil pusher if there ever was one. "We don't have anyone else who combines your background in history and behavioral analysis. You're a good fit. We also feel …" he gave a sharp glance at Bradshaw, who shifted uncomfortably in his seat "… that the Behavioral Analysis Unit could do with a lighter touch."

Daniel leaned back, all the fight gone out of him. So there it was. All those disciplinary reports, all those complaints from perps and witnesses. They'd all finally added up. He was getting transferred from one of the FBI's most important and prestigious divisions to some new office that probably had little funding and zero prestige.

The Deputy Director leaned forward. "You'll be flying to Philadelphia this afternoon. Mrs. Whitaker will email you all the travel details and contacts in Philly. Study those case files. We feel the killer might strike again, and soon. You need to get him before he does."

"This is a chance to make good on the ground floor of a new division," Ochiai said in her Texas drawl. "It's a great opportunity for you."

Make good? Yeah, right. I'm being demoted.

There was nothing more to say, so Daniel said nothing. He gathered his files, thanked the bigwigs in as sincere a tone as he could muster, and headed out.

He closed the door behind him, closing the door on a successful career as he did so. He'd caught three serial killers in the past four years, saving countless lives, and this was how they repaid him?

Daniel knew he could be hard to work with. He knew he shouldn't snap at his superiors or show up his coworkers, but he saved lives damn it!

Daniel walked up to Flora Whitaker's desk like a chastened schoolboy. She was busy typing on her computer.

"You have some travel documents for me?" he asked.

"I'll send them over," Whitaker said, still typing. "Go home and pack. Your flight is at two."

"New division," Daniel grunted, trying to get a response from her. Maybe she knew something the others hadn't let on.

She looked up briefly. "It's not a demotion."

She got back to her typing.

"You could have fooled me," Daniel growled, stalking out the door.

The moment he stepped out, his phone rang. His wife Veronica. Daniel groaned.

Just when he thought the day couldn't get any worse.

CHAPTER TWO

"Did you get the papers?" Veronica asked when he picked up. Most wives started with "hello." Even strangers did that.

Sadly, she was becoming a stranger. More and more every month.

"Hello," Daniel said, his heart sinking. He walked down the hall, eyes darting to the left and right, hoping none of the other agents passing by could see his stress. An office environment where everyone was trained to read body language made it hard to have private phone calls. Daniel headed for the bathroom.

"Hello," Veronica replied with obvious impatience. "I asked if you got the papers."

"Just a minute. I'm in the hallway. Hold on."

Daniel hurried to the nearest bathroom, only to see a guy go in just in front of him.

So much for privacy.

Between the men's and women's room was the door to the disabled bathroom. Glancing to make sure no one was looking, he went in there and locked the door.

It was a small room with only one toilet. He sat on the lid, leaned against the handrail, and said, "Yes, I got the papers. I haven't read them."

"Because you're too busy with a case," Veronica said this like she'd said it a thousand times before. In fact, she had.

"No, it's because I know what they say, and I don't want to sign them."

Deep sigh. "Look, Daniel. I can get a divorce with or without your consent. I'm trying to be nice here."

"And I'm trying to save our marriage!"

"You're years too late for that."

"It's never too late," Daniel said, checking his watch. He had a plane to catch, and barely enough time to get home, pack, and get to the airport. Those tricky bastards hadn't given him enough time to fight this.

"Come on, Daniel. Just sign the papers. I've been very generous with the alimony payments."

She had. That wasn't the point, though. He wanted a wife, not an ex.

"Look, honey, I know we've had problems, but we can work them out. We don't want to throw away eight years—"

"Seven and a half."

Daniel gnashed his teeth. Veronica was a math professor at Georgetown. Always precise. Always analytical. Always correcting him.

"Whatever. The point is we don't want to throw that away."

Another deep sigh. "I want to move on. I'm not getting any younger."

"Yeah, about that. I talked to the adoption agency and—"

"We've had this conversation."

"Yeah, but listen. They say they can get us a baby in less than a year. They say our income and my career in law enforcement means we get priority."

"I don't want someone else's baby. I want my own."

"A baby is a baby. What difference does it make?"

"Why do men always say that!"

Daniel cursed silently to himself. He had blundered. He'd said that once before and Veronica had blown up, and now he had stuck his foot in it again.

For a moment there was silence, then Veronica went on, her voice wavering.

"I'm tired of this, Daniel. I'm tired of you running off on cases all the time. I'm tired of you not getting why I want a baby. I'm tired of you being so insensitive."

"I'm not insensitive. I'm trying to give you what you want."

Pause. "You can't."

Veronica hung up.

Daniel slumped on the toilet, hanging his head.

"That wasn't fair," he whispered.

He sat there, staring at the floor, resisting the urge to bash his head against the wall.

Daniel glanced at his watch.

"Crap," he muttered.

He pulled himself together and opened the door, only to find a female agent in a wheelchair on the other side.

She frowned. “This bathroom is for disabled people.”

“Well, my wife always says I’m an emotional cripple.”

The frown deepened. “I don’t appreciate that term.”

“Blame her,” he snapped. “I got a plane to catch.”

* * *

The CSI team had already come and gone from the crime scene. Now all that was left was the broken bust and a chalk outline showing where Ted Peterson had lain drowning in his own blood.

A dried pool of that blood, sickeningly large, took up much of the landing of the stairwell.

Daniel stood with a Philadelphia homicide detective and the museum director. Homicide Detective Philip Fish was a stooped older man with a sad, tired look to him. His sagging face under heavy brows had a beaten look to it, like life had bludgeoned him to the ground and, once he was there, kicked him.

In other words, he looked like Daniel felt.

The museum director, a Mr. Farnsworth (no first name offered), was a stout middle-aged man with a ruddy face and designer suit. He smelled of inherited wealth and thirty-year-old Scotch.

“So we checked on Peterson’s background,” Detective Fish told him. “He mostly kept to himself. No known enemies. No convictions or arrests. Nothing illegal found in his apartment.”

“He was a quiet man,” Museum Director Farnsworth said. “Not very educated, so this job was a bit lost on him, but he was a reliable employee. Everybody liked him.”

“What about his Internet history?” Daniel asked the Philly homicide detective.

“Cybercrime is searching through his Internet history right now,” Detective Fish replied. “I doubt we’ll find anything though, judging from what his friends and neighbors say.”

The museum director shook his head. “You won’t find anything. He was such a quiet man. Fred wouldn’t hurt a fly.”

“Ted,” Daniel corrected, and turned back to the detective. “CSI get anything?”

The detective shrugged. "This is a public venue. That bannister over there is covered in prints. We also retrieved plenty of hair and skin samples. Unless we nab a suspect, all those samples won't do much good, and any halfway decent defense lawyer would just say the guy visited the museum."

Daniel grunted. That was always a problem with murders in public places. "What about the door where he came in?"

"We had some luck there. The lawn he crossed had just been watered, so he got a bit of dirt on the soles of his boots. We got a print at the doorstep. Also, a couple of flakes of clay. CSI isn't clear if he had been working with clay or had been walking through a place with clay like a dried streambed. They'll know more once they'd put it through the lab."

"Well, that's something at least." Daniel turned to the director. "Mr. Farnsworth, are you sure nothing was stolen?"

"Quite sure. We did a complete inventory. The only thing that was broken was this bust, which is of no real value. It's a plaster bust made in the 1930s by an art student, who donated it to the museum. It's of Edward Gibbon. He was the author of—"

"*The Decline and Fall of the Roman Empire*. I've read it."

Mr. Farnsworth looked surprised. Daniel tried to hide his irritation. Why did everyone think people from law enforcement were semiliterate?

Daniel took a slow turn around the broken bust, taking care not to step on the giant scab that was once the lifeblood of poor Ted Peterson.

"So this bust isn't valuable," Daniel said.

"Not in any real sense," the director said. "In fact, of all the *objets d'art* in the museum, the murderer chose the least valuable one to destroy."

Daniel flicked him an annoyed glance. Daniel might have been educated, but he didn't like the kind of people who used foreign terms like *"objets d'art"* in casual conversation. It made him feel like kicking them in the *testicoli*, as his partner would say.

Or ex-partner, as the FBI thought she was.

They had another think coming.

Something odd caught his eye. Two of the larger pieces showed there had been a hollow space inside the bust.

He squatted down to get a better look.

"This bust was hollow," Daniel said.

Mr. Farnsworth shrugged. “Plaster busts are often hollow. It’s a brittle material and making it hollow with a bit of wiring or other armature in the interior strengthens the matrix.”

“There’s no armature on the inside.”

“That isn’t always required. It’s life sized, and only the bust. A full statue would require it.”

Daniel studied it for a moment longer, leaning in closer. There was a small dot on the smooth side of one portion of the hollow, shiny and green, barely a quarter of an inch in diameter.

“What’s that?” Daniel asked.

“No idea,” Detective Fish said, peering over his shoulder.

Museum Director Farnsworth, unable to think of something clever, said nothing.

“We’ll take it to the lab,” the detective said. “Hey, there’s another.”

He pointed to another fragment that had an identical dot.

Daniel gave the detective an appreciative nod, then moved around the bust, studying it from all angles, especially the remains of the cyst that had been inside it, and found several more identical dots.

“That’s unusual,” Farnsworth murmured.

“What?” Daniel asked.

The museum director pointed to the base of the bust, which had broken into two halves.

“There’s no hole in the base. When a plaster bust has a hollow core, there’s always a hole in the base. The artist works the plaster around a shaped core stuck to a working surface, and that leaves a hole in the base that cannot be seen when the bust is standing upright.”

Daniel, squatting near the base, absentmindedly tapped his thumb against his knee. He felt that delicious prickle of excitement he always got when he had discovered something significant.

“So whoever made this bust didn’t want anyone to know it was hollow. And I’ll bet my left nut that the little stains I spotted were made by whatever was inside. Seems to me your murderer knew something about your collection you didn’t.”

Farnsworth looked insulted.

Daniel stood. “Looks like we’re done here.”

“Who do you think murdered Fred?” Farnsworth asked.

Daniel glared at him. “His name was Ted.” Farnsworth blinked and gave an almost imperceptible shrug. Daniel turned his back on him.

While Detective Fish bagged the fragments of the bust, Daniel moved through the museum, retracing the security guard's steps. He walked a set path through the museum that the director had told Daniel about, so he most likely had passed through the Italian Renaissance room last, and before that the Great Hall.

Daniel had looked at some photos of the hall on the Internet while waiting to board his flight, but that didn't prepare him for the soaring roof with its intricately painted arches of gold and blue Celtic knotwork, its collection of medieval armaments, and its stunning stained-glass windows shining in the bright sunlight of a cloudless spring afternoon.

The place was probably crowded on a normal day, but since the museum had been closed because of the murder, he had the room all to himself. It was quiet here. Peaceful. Poor Ted Peterson probably loved wandering through these halls at night. The detective said his apartment was filled with history and art books. Despite what that asshole director thought, Daniel figured Ted probably knew about every object in this place.

Had he known the bust of Edward Gibbon was hollow?

Probably not. There was no way to tell just by looking at it from the outside. And Daniel bet whatever was hidden in the cyst hadn't rattled when the bust was moved, assuming it ever was moved since its donation more than a century ago. There were enough points of contact on the inside of the cyst that the object was probably stuck in place. Probably no one associated with the museum would have known anything was hidden inside.

So how had the murderer known?

And why kill the security guard? The killer hadn't alerted Peterson when he broke into the building, or the murder would have taken place downstairs. Instead, the most likely scenario was that the killer broke the bust to retrieve whatever was inside, and Peterson came running.

So Ted Peterson hadn't known the killer had broken into the museum until that moment. The killer must have known there was a security guard on the premises, though. He had come too well prepared not to. He had known the layout and known the security system. This old building, with all its rooms and stairs, offered dozens of hiding places. The killer could have waited as Peterson had passed by one his rounds, waited until Peterson was at the other end of the building, and then smashed the bust. Peterson might have not even heard, and even if he did, the killer could have been long gone by the time the security guard showed up.

There was no reason to kill the security guard at all, which meant the killer wanted to kill him.

So which was more important—stealing whatever was inside that bust or killing the man who guarded it? Or were they two halves of the same goal?

The break-in at the Cloisters had been similar. In that situation, there had been two security guards, one on the grounds and one inside. The killer had waited until the outside security guard had been on the other end of the property before moving in. Then he had disabled the cameras, picked the lock, and disabled the security system.

After that, the killer's movements were unclear, but ended in breaking into a display case holding an ivory figurine, snapping the figurine in half, and then killing the security guard close by. Probably when the guard heard the noise and came to investigate.

Interestingly, both guards at the Cloisters carried walkie talkies. The interior guard hadn't radioed to his coworker, meaning he didn't have time to. Once again, the killer had been in a large building with plenty of places to hide and had waited until the guard was close before killing him. He could have avoided the guard entirely, but instead chose to add murder to destruction of property.

Why?

Daniel opened his briefcase and pulled out the report from the Cloisters, flipping to the photos of the ivory figurine. It showed a Virgin Mary holding a baby Jesus, snapped in half, probably by smacking it against the base of the display case. The description written by the investigator at the scene said it dated to the fourteenth century.

That would make it valuable, although tricky to sell since it was easily identifiable. Of course, in the seamy underbelly of the antiquities market there were plenty of customers willing to buy stolen artifacts for their private collections.

But the killer hadn't stolen it. He had broken it. He had broken an all-but-worthless plaster bust too.

When Daniel turned the page to the next photo, his eyes bugged.

There was a hole in the bottom of the figurine.

It didn't look very big, but it looked drilled rather than the result of breakage. What was that doing there?

Two museum objects with holes inside broken by the same killer. That was too much of a coincidence to be a coincidence. He was looking for something.

But the hole in the Virgin Mary figurine looked tiny, less than a quarter of an inch in diameter. Could you really hide something in there, and keep it hidden?

Daniel had no answer to that. All those European tours Mom had taken him on and his undergraduate degree weren't enough for him to cough up solutions to this riddle.

He needed to find an expert.

CHAPTER THREE

Georgetown University
The next day

"So, as we can see, the scribes and scholars of the High Middle Ages used a variety of secret codes in order to communicate with one another. The Seville Manuscript uses the same type of code as the Turin Fragment. This particular code was broken four years ago by myself and Dr. Luis Hidalgo."

Professor Remi Laurent flicked on another slide from her PowerPoint presentation. She dressed conservatively, in a white shirt and tan slacks, her long black hair reaching to her middle back. She had the high cheekbones, delicate features, and blue eyes of the French upper class from which she sprang, and a youthful appearance that, despite her 38 years, made her look not much older than the twenty-something graduate students taking up the front row.

She stood at a lectern in front of a class of about thirty students, both advanced undergraduates and a few graduate students attending her course "History 330: Codes, Ciphers, and Hidden Messages in Medieval and Renaissance Texts and Art." This particular lecture was on late medieval codes used in secret correspondence between scholars.

The slide showed a sheet of parchment from Turin dated to 1285. Remi looked at it as if seeing a picture of an old friend. In many ways it was. She had spent more time with it than she had with most humans in her life and found the interaction far more rewarding.

The parchment looked like a regular letter written in the standard Latin of the period, until one got to the final few paragraphs, where the letters all appeared scrambled.

"At the bottom of this letter, which discusses the functions of a monastery near Turin, you will see that the Latin turns to gibberish."

At least she hoped her students saw that. Most looked like they were zoning out as they did during all her lectures. Pretending not to notice, she went on.

"This gibberish is actually a code. It's a simple type of code called a Caesar cipher, although with a special twist. In a Caesar cipher, each letter is replaced by the letter three letters further on in the alphabet. So A becomes D, D becomes G, etc. For the final letters of the alphabet, it loops around, so Z become C.

"The Caesar cipher was pretty well-known during the Middle Ages and Renaissance, so our two correspondents added a variation to make it harder to crack. Instead of the traditional three places, they made it five. Now you might wonder how each person would know this since they lived in different countries and had never actually met. That's where they got clever. At the top of one letter, you see this crude drawing of a hand. Five fingers. It was also dated the fifth of May, the fifth month, and yet the uncoded part of the letter mentions the writer had just celebrated the Feast of Saint John the Baptist, which is on June 23. Thus, he draws the reader's attention to the incorrect date. This is how the reader was able to crack the code, and it's how we cracked the code too."

Remi allowed herself a moment of serene pleasure. She always loved solving puzzles and solving a puzzle from centuries ago was one of the greatest thrills she had ever known. Another great thrill was imparting that enjoyment to other people.

Back at the Sorbonne she had a sizeable following of students who eagerly attended her every lecture and lapped up her every article. The give and take she enjoyed with them in their countless conversations acted like fuel, driving her on to more and more research.

"Now you might be wondering what was hidden in this message. Military secrets? Instructions to poison a nobleman? Directions to buried treasure? Nothing so dramatic as that. It's a series of jokes about priests and their mistresses."

This brought scattered laughter from the audience. Turned out some of the students had a pulse after all.

One of the young men, a graduate student, raised his hand.

"Yes?" Remi couldn't remember his name. He had never approached her to talk. Few of them had.

"Could you tell us some of the jokes?" he asked with a grin.

"Maybe a bit too risqué for class," she replied, remembering what the dean and the department head had told her when she came for the start of her visiting year.

This is America, not France. Students are more sensitive.

"Just one," the graduate student persisted. One of the girls shot him an angry glance.

"If you want to read them for yourself, there are some examples in my and Dr. Hidalgo's article in the *Journal of Medieval Studies* from 2015. You can look it up on JSTOR."

The graduate student wrote that down while the female student who had been frowning raised her hand.

"Yes?" Remi asked, against her better judgement.

"Don't you think posting a link to such material on a university website constitutes support for sexist jokes?"

Good Lord, they were written centuries ago.

"No," Remi replied.

"But don't you think—"

"You don't have to read them if you don't want to."

Silence.

Professor Remi Laurent looked out over her class. Except for a few somewhat eager graduate students in the front row, the sea of American faces looked impassive, bored even. You'd think that secret codes and naughty stories about priests would pique their interest, but no. It seemed nothing could get these young people excited except flirting and being offended and staring at their phones.

The Sorbonne was so different. As the apex of the French educational system, no one got in there unless they proved themselves the most serious among scholars. Everyone in her lectures back home listened to her with rapt attention and assailed her during office hours with intelligent questions and requests for more reading.

Not here. The only people who came to her office hours were students who thought whining for an extension for their assignments would work better in person than via email.

At least here the department respected her studies into the esoteric side of history. They had always poo-pooed that in Paris. She had to endure countless snide comments at faculty meetings, lack of mention of her latest publications in the faculty newsletter, and the scheduling of her classes at inconvenient times. It was a testament to her students' loyalty that they would come at 8am on a Monday or 4pm on a Friday.

Georgetown was the reverse. The faculty loved her research and even arranged interviews on TV and radio when she first came, but the students couldn't care less.

Remi clicked onto the next slide, showing a medieval parchment punctured by several holes from bookworms. The writing was a strange combination of Latin and Greek letters, plus several invented symbols.

"Now this next code was far more difficult to crack, and hid a far more interesting message, one that changed the course of French history. The king—"

The door at the back of the lecture hall banged open and a tall man about her age with broad shoulders but a rather soft middle entered. He wore a black suit and tie. His face bore a frown under brown hair cut short. He looked right at her with hard brown eyes that expressed impatience.

"Professor Remi Laurent?"

Remi blinked. "Yes?"

"Agent Daniel Walker, FBI," he said, producing a badge she couldn't make out from across the room. "I need to speak with you."

The class stirred, everyone craning their necks to stare at the newcomer.

"I'm giving a lecture," she said uncertainly. *FBI? What are they doing here? Something go wrong with my work visa? But they wouldn't send the FBI, would they?*

"The lecture can wait. We don't have much time."

"Is Professor Laurent under arrest?" one of the girls asked.

"No," he said.

Remi flicked to the next slide in her lecture, rattled but trying not to show it. She had no idea what this could be about. All she knew was that this FBI agent was irritating in the extreme. If she wasn't a suspect in some terrorism incident or something, why barge in here like that?

"I'm very glad to hear I won't be seeing the inside of an American prison. That means this can wait until after my lecture. Now as I was saying—"

"I need to speak with you," the agent snapped. "*Now.*"

Remi frowned at the FBI agent. "You're out of line."

"So flunk me. But first you and I need to talk."

More murmuring from the class. She'd completely lost their attention. Getting it back would take half the period.

"Stay here," she told them, stepping out from behind the lectern. "I'll be back in a minute."

"No, you will not be back in a minute," Agent Walker grumbled. He walked down the aisle, clapping his hands. "OK, kiddies. Class dismissed! Me and the professor have some things to talk about and I don't have time for any crap from any of you."

"Is she under arrest?" one of the students asked.

"No, but you all will be if you don't clear out of here. MOVE!"

The students hurried out of the lecture hall like a pack of lemmings.

Remi left the lectern and stomped up the aisle to the agent, fuming.

"How dare you! You can't do this!" she shouted as the students streamed past him, headed for the exit. They didn't need much convincing. Maybe she was a boring lecturer.

"I just did," he said, giving her a smug smile that she would have liked to slap off his face.

Not that she ever resorted to violence. Certainly not with an officer of the law.

The last student fled, and the door banged shut.

"What's all this about?" Remi demanded.

Agent Walker pulled out his phone and tapped on the gallery. He held the phone up to show her a close-up photo of a man lying dead on the floor. His half-severed neck, clotted with a mass of blood, took up center frame.

Remi's stomach roiled. She raised her hands and turned away. "Augh! What are you doing?"

"This has happened twice now. I need your help to stop it from happening again."

"That's horrible!" Remi sobbed, burying her face in her hands. Her shoulders trembled. She staggered to the nearest seat and sat down hard. Why would he show her such a disgusting image?

Remi heard him sit down beside her and she edged away.

"Sorry for putting you through that," he said softly. Remi heard a surprising amount of sympathy in his voice. "That man was a security guard, killed last night in the Glencairn Museum. I'm sure you're familiar with the place. The night before, a security guard was killed under similar circumstances at the Cloisters. That's two nights in a row. Last night he skipped. That means either he's planning his next break-in or he's traveling to some place more distant. It's only a five-and-a-half-hour drive from the Cloisters to the Glencairn Museum. Maybe his next hit is in Los Angeles or someplace. Maybe even overseas. That's why I need your help *now*."

That made Remi sit up and wipe her eyes. Why her? She took a cautious glance to make sure he had put his phone away, and then turned to him.

The FBI agent looked at her with a serious expression. Now that she was closer, she could see he had a haggard look. Something beyond tired, more like haunted. Those brown eyes, a bit bloodshot, were open too wide and blinked too little, as if he had just seen that picture on his phone for the first time, as if he was constantly seeing it for the first time.

"I-I read about that break in at the Cloisters," Remi said. "The guard caught the man trying to steal a medieval ivory and the thief panicked and killed the guard, running off without stealing anything. Are you saying he's struck again in Pennsylvania?"

"The newspapers didn't get the whole story, as usual. At the Cloisters, the intruder went in and broke an ivory figurine of the Virgin Mary holding Christ. We believe the noise brought the security guard running, at which point the intruder slit his throat. At the Glencairn Museum, the intruder broke in, smashed a twentieth century bust of Edward Gibbon, and then slit the guard's throat when he arrived on the scene. In neither case did the intruder steal anything, and in both cases, he could have waited until the guard was out of earshot before doing his vandalism."

"So you think this is the same man?" A rising suspicion of a motive pushed itself into Remi's consciousness. It seemed too crazy to take seriously, but she could not shake it.

"We have security video of what looks to be the same man. In both cases he picked the lock on a door and disabled the alarm and security cameras. It has to be the same guy. It got me to wondering why he targeted those museums and that got me to researching what those museums had in common."

Remi's heart was pounding hard now. In a tremulous voice she said, "And that led you to me and my research into the cryptex."

Agent Daniel Walker nodded, and all of Remi Laurcnt's hopes were fulfilled.

And all of her fears.

CHAPTER FOUR

Daniel felt adrenaline pulse in his veins. This hunch about Professor Laurent had turned out to be correct, like all his hunches did. The professor had perked up, outrage turned to excitement, making Daniel feel sure he had scored a hit.

He was good at what he did. Nothing felt more fulfilling than tracking down a killer.

"So you've heard of the cryptex?" she asked. "You know of my research?"

"Yeah. After the second murder, I searched the Internet for info about secrets or treasure hidden in medieval art collections. He isn't the typical thief. He could have taken any number of priceless artifacts and didn't. He was looking for something hidden. It didn't take long to find you and your research into that cryptex thing. I want to talk to you about it."

"What did your research tell you?" Professor Laurent asked. For a moment Daniel felt like a student getting a pop quiz.

"It's sort of an early version of the Rubik's cube. A series of ivory cubes all connected that have letters and numbers on them. It supposedly held great secrets if someone could crack the code and open it."

"What did you think of that?"

"Well, I got to admit I began to get bored. It sounded like a conspiracy theory cooked up by Internet addicts who have bad spelling and write in all caps. But then I found you, a real academic from a top university who took it seriously. That made me think it's real."

"It is real."

Did he detect a note of defensiveness in her response? Maybe she got ragged by some of her colleagues. It was a bit of a wacko subject, after all.

Probably a good idea not to ruffle her feathers too much.

Oh, I already did by bursting into her class.

Classy as usual, Danny boy.

"As an investigator I suspend judgement on that sort of thing. I got to admit, the idea of some secret device with technology way before its time holding secrets people are willing to kill for seems like a stretch, but it doesn't matter whether this cryptex thing exists as long as the killer believes it does."

The professor studied him. "But why do you think the killer isn't just some psychotic or failed thief? Why link it to the cryptex at all?"

"He's a damn good burglar. Disconnected some top-notch security systems and knew the rounds of the security guards so he could slip past them. He could have easily stolen something. Instead, he just broke things."

"Hidden in medieval art collections …" she whispered.

Those lovely blue eyes lost focus and her lips moved slightly. Daniel started to say something, then stopped himself. She was working things out. Daniel let her do it. You never interrupted a potential asset when they were thinking things through.

Professor Laurent continued to look off into space, lips moving slightly. It had been several seconds now, and she showed no signs of stopping.

Weird. But judging from her CV she was a genius, and geniuses were always weird. He had met a few in the course of his work. Most of them had been serial killers, of course, but the law-abiding geniuses were just as strange.

Daniel felt a pang of regret and pity for showing this bookish woman that photo of poor Ted Peterson. He hated showing civilians the ugliness and filth he had to wallow in for the sake of his job. Sometimes, though, it was necessary to get them to understand what was at stake.

That drug dealer hadn't been affected at all when Daniel showed him pictures of Finger Man's victims. The scumbag had been selling steroids to some of the victims and perhaps the murderer too but wouldn't talk because he wanted to protect himself. Even seeing those dead young men with missing fingers hadn't moved him.

That's why Daniel had stuck the bastard's head into a toilet and flushed.

He wanted to treat this professor differently. He wanted to put a protective arm around her and tell her everything would be all right, that after the interview she could go back to her cozy little academic life.

But he couldn't do that. The killer was out there, and they needed to find him.

At last Professor Laurent spoke.

"You should check if the bust is hollow."

Daniel's heart skipped a beat. "It was."

"And the ivory figurine, it had a hole drilled through the bottom, didn't it?"

"It did! How did you know that?"

"Medieval ivory figurines often had a hole drilled into the bottom so they could be set on a metal dowel in order to be displayed. I bet there was a metal dowel in the display case it came from." Daniel nodded, even more certain now that he made the right call in coming here. "The hole was probably original. It's too risky to drill a hole in a fragile artifact like that. Did you shine a light or send a wire down the hole to measure it?"

"Um, no," Daniel replied, feeling foolish.

"If you do, I'll bet you'll find the hole is longer than the dowel in the display case. Something was hidden in there, just like something was hidden in the bust of Edward Gibbon."

"So he snapped the figurine in half to get what was inside?"

Professor Laurent didn't reply. Her eyes had unfocused again, lips moving silently. Her hands moved too, seeming to measure dimensions in the air.

What a weirdo. At least she's a useful weirdo. What could have been in that figurine?

Daniel thought for a second. He couldn't imagine anything could be hidden inside that little hole except a rolled-up piece of paper. What could that have been? A treasure map? Instructions to the location of another object? The combination to a safe?

Professor Laurent smacked the wooden desk with the flat of her palm, making Daniel jump, and sprang to her feet.

"The bust contained the dodecahedron!"

Daniel blinked. "The what?"

"The Gorizia dodecahedron."

"Catch me up, professor," he said, trying not to let his impatience leak into his voice.

"It's a twelve-sided object made of copper, built in the—"

"Wait, did you say copper? We found green stains inside the hollow of the bust."

"YES!" she shouted, pumping her fists in the air like she'd just made a touchdown. "That's from the points. They were small and round, right, like dots?"

Her enthusiasm was infectious. Daniel stood up too.

"Yeah. So what was this Gorizia thing?"

"A class of ancient Roman artifact. They are copper polyhedrons with twelve sides. They're hollow with holes in each face, and little round knobs on the corners."

Daniel's brow furrowed. "What the hell were they for?"

Professor Laurent smiled. "That's a good question. Nobody knows."

"But I thought the cryptex was made in the Middle Ages. Why would a do-whatever—"

"Dodecahedron."

"—have anything to do with it?"

"Early scholars think the dodecahedron was used in Roman magic. That may be so. One found in Gorizia in northern Italy was used, according to some sources, as a sort of clue to unlocking the cryptex. The code for the cryptex was based on the proportions of the Gorizia dodecahedron in some way."

"What way?"

Professor Laurent shrugged. "Nobody knows."

Daniel felt disappointed. Just how much did this world-class expert *not* know?

"Wait. If you don't know, how would the killer?"

"Maybe he's discovered something we haven't. Or maybe he hasn't and will keep on killing until he does. Whatever his plans are, that Roman artifact is vital to unlocking the cryptex. It went missing, sold at auction to an anonymous buyer, more than a century ago. If your murderer has got his hands on it, he's close. Very close."

Daniel raised his hands in a calming gesture. "OK, that's great. You're already helping a lot. But I need to be brought up to speed. We're jumping around here. Tell me more about this cryptex thing. It's attracted a lot of kooks online." Professor Laurent gave him an irritated look. He hastened to add, "Not saying you're a kook, but some of the people this story attracts certainly are." The woman nodded. Surely, she must have seen this herself. "Now I've read a bit about this thing, but I need to know more if I'm going to find the killer. There's too much online to sort through."

"There are better sources of information than the Internet."

"Yeah. You."

Professor Laurent took a deep breath and sat. Daniel sat too.

Eyes sparking with enthusiasm, the professor began.

"The cryptex is a unique medieval artifact that most scholars don't even think ever existed, but it's captured the imagination of generations of mystics, oddballs, treasure hunters, and conspiracy theorists."

"And one serious academic."

"Yeah," she said with a grin, and Daniel knew he had been forgiven for his remark about kooks. "As you said, the cryptex looked a bit like a low-tech, rectangular Rubik's cube. It was a series of interconnected ivory cubes with numbers and letters engraved on each surface. The story was that if it was turned to the right combination it would open up to reveal … something."

"Something?"

"Sadly, that's where consensus about the cryptex stops. Nobody knows who created it or when, and nobody knows where it is. Most scholars don't even think it exists, dismissing it as a medieval fable like the unicorn or the Blemmyae."

Daniel had no idea what a Blemmyae was but decided not to interrupt. He could Google it later, assuming he could figure out how to spell it.

"But people have hunted for it for centuries," the professor continued, "hunted for clues to its location hidden in *objets d'art*."

Oh God, she uses snooty terms too. Well, of course she does.

What she said next certainly got his attention.

"This isn't the first time someone has killed for it."

Daniel perked up. "What? There's been other murders?"

Professor Laurent waved a dismissive hand. "Far too late for you to solve. The latest happened in the 1920s, but it just goes to show how serious some of those who hunt for the cryptex can be."

"You can tell me about those murders later. So why would someone kill for it? Because it holds the secrets to the universe or something?"

"Some think so, especially the fringe researchers. I am the only serious scholar of my generation to write about it."

"Yeah, I noticed that. Do you get flak from your colleagues for the company you keep?"

Professor Laurent winced. "Yes, I do. Mainstream scholarship thinks it's just an old story. I'm convinced it existed. I've read enough textual mentions in Italian, Byzantine, Jewish, and French sources to take the idea seriously. The cryptex appears to have been constructed in the final years of the thirteenth century, in either Byzantium or northern Italy, during the first glimmerings of what would in the following century become the Renaissance."

"Byzantium? That was the Eastern Roman Empire, right?"

"Yes, its capital was Constantinople, now Istanbul, and it lasted until 1453. Byzantium retained much Classic knowledge and created some impressive technical feats such as steam engines that made golden birds sing and thrones rise to the ceiling. Greek Fire, a form of napalm, destroyed the navies of their enemies. Their medical texts were far in advance of anything in Europe and rivaled those of the great Abbasid Caliphate. If any culture had the ability to create something like the cryptex, it would have been the Byzantines."

A distant memory from his childhood came back to him. He stood with his mother and his mother's new boyfriend, who he had been instructed to call Uncle Ray, in the Basilica of San Vitale in Ravenna. Young Daniel—he remembered he was about ten or so—stared in wonder at the gold mosaics covering the interior of the domes. They gleamed in the candlelight with a warm glow, the dark figures of Jesus and the saints seeming to hover suspended in front of the gold background.

"Wow," was all Daniel could say.

Mom clicked her tongue. "I was hoping you'd have something more intelligent to say than that."

"It's cool looking," Daniel ventured, looking for approval in her face and not seeing any. "Like, all the gold and stuff."

Mom shook her head and sighed. Daniel slumped, knowing he had failed her again.

She raised her Pentax and took a couple of shots, then moved away, camera in hand, to take a shot in another room. Uncle Ray put an arm around Daniel's shoulder.

"Look at that writing up there made up of mosaic tiles. You've been studying Latin. Can you read that?"

"That's not Latin, that's Greek."

"That's right! The Byzantines spoke Greek, not Latin. You spotted that pretty quick."

Daniel grinned. Uncle Ray paid a lot of attention to him, at least when he wasn't kissing Mom.

"Yeah, I could spot that wasn't Latin. No way!"

Uncle Ray glanced over his shoulder, then hugged Daniel closer. "What a smart little boy you are ..."

"You alright?"

Professor Laurent's question snapped him out of his thoughts. She looked at him with that penetrating stare of hers.

"Um, yeah. I was just ... thinking. The Byzantines spoke Greek, right? All the sources say the letters on the cryptex are in Latin."

The professor smiled. "Rare knowledge for a policeman. Looks like someone educated you when you were younger."

Daniel looked at the floor.

"You could say that," he mumbled.

"You're quite right. My personal theory is that it was created in Italy. The two cultures shared a lot of technology. Many Byzantine scholars fled to Italy as their empire crumbled in the face of the Muslim advance."

"And what do these sources say about what's inside?" Daniel asked, forcing himself to focus on the case. It helped. Mostly.

The professor grimaced. "Frustratingly little. One undated scrap of vellum from Ravenna spoke of it being a 'mystical device to unlock the secrets of the universe.' A passing reference in the margins of a 15th century Byzantine Bible referred to it as 'the puzzle of wisdom.' A Hebrew manuscript written in 1601, in Tangier, referred to it as the "Lost Key of Solomon.'"

"Sounds like something a deranged mind would be willing to kill for. Perhaps a religious fanatic."

He'd hunted down one of those a few years back. A defrocked priest who had gone on a spree, sleeping with prostitutes and killing them because they were "evil temptresses." The guy was in prison for life now, trying to convince any inmate who'd listen that it was all the hookers' fault.

The professor nodded. "A religious fundamentalist or mystic would fit. People of that sort have been looking for it for centuries. Sources from the Enlightenment and modern periods say the cryptex was hidden to keep its secret safe, and that clues to its location had been scattered around the world, awaiting the one wise enough to find them."

"So no one has ever been able to crack the code?"

"No one."

Daniel gave a little shrug and an abashed smile. "I never solved the Rubik's Cube either."

"I can solve the standard three-by-three model in 6.2 seconds. The four-by-four in one minute and seven seconds."

"Well la dee da."

Professor Laurent grinned. "Don't feel insecure. I have a natural talent for puzzles. Always have."

"Wait. Why not just bust the thing open to see what's inside?"

"Is that what you did with your Rubik's Cube?"

"No. I switched all the stickers, so it looked like I solved it," Daniel admitted.

They both laughed. She was cute when she laughed. Compelling when she was serious. Quite an interesting woman.

Focus.

"I've spent much of my career tracking down references to the cryptex, some of them obscure and many of them fantastical. The earliest, most serious ones, while claiming it held mystical secrets, agree that it had a more mundane function. The code kept it locked, and whatever was hidden inside would be lost if the device was simply broken open. I believe the cubes that make up the cryptex probably have another set of letters on the inside, and that the code would make the cryptex open up to reveal a message."

"Any idea what the message is?"

She shrugged. "What I wouldn't give to know."

"Any idea where the killer might strike next? Or does he have all the clues already?"

"I don't think he has all the clues. Sources differ, but several clues were spread out across the world in order to ensure their safety. There's no telling where he could strike next …" Professor Laurent faded off again, but she didn't seem to be thinking, she seemed to be terrified, like when he inflicted that photo on her.

Suddenly she sprang out of her seat, dragging Daniel to his feet with her.

"Oh my God, I know where he's going to strike next!"

"Where?"

Could it be this easy?

"Right here in D.C., at The Twenty-First Century Museum of Culture."

"Why there?"

"The cryptex hasn't been seen for centuries, but back at the turn of the last century, a group of millionaires and antiquarians who called themselves the Cryptex Club collected clues to its whereabouts. Some of these were ancient objects like the Gorizia dodecahedron. Others were bits of medieval manuscript. They got close to finding the cryptex, but something stopped them. No one knows exactly what. Perhaps they had a falling out, or perhaps they were missing a final, vital clue. I think that's the more likely explanation because they cooperated enough to hide the clues in various places.

"The millionaires in the club sponsored the founding of several large museums to hide the clues in the collections. Raymond Pitcairn and his wife Mildred Glenn had suffered a couple of break-ins at their mansion from someone looking for the pieces of the puzzle they had been keeping, so they founded the Glencairn Museum figuring it would be a less likely target. George Grey Barnard and John D. Rockefeller founded the Cloisters for the same reason. A thief wouldn't expect them to hide the clues in plain sight."

"The Purloined Letter," Agent Walker said with a chuckle.

The professor smiled. "You like Poe?"

"Loved him as a kid. Gave me the creeps."

"I liked him too." That made Daniel feel good. The professor went on. "So the collectors founded museums and galleries, or donated collections of objects to existing museums."

"But this museum you're talking about was only founded three years ago. It was all over the news," Daniel objected.

"Yes, but there's a visiting exhibition there right now of artifacts from the Cluny Museum in Paris. That's a museum devoted to medieval art," the professor explained.

"I know, I've been there, go on," Daniel said impatiently. These academic types took too damn long to get to the point.

Professor Laurent blinked in surprise, then continued.

"The exhibition included the complete collection of artifacts donated to the Cluny by the Compte de Lacy in 1908. He was the last of his line and donated his entire collection of medieval art to the Cluny. I believe he was a member of this international society I mentioned."

"So one of the clues might be hidden in one of the artifacts?"

The professor nodded, her face practically glowing with excitement. Daniel felt his skin prickle. They might be able to bust this freak tonight.

Daniel pulled out his phone and looked up the museum.

"I'll call the museum and make them aware of the situation," Daniel said. "The guy only hits after dark so we shouldn't tell them to close early. He might be watching and that will only make him suspicious. Oh, I see they don't close for three hours. That gives me time to get a team together and get in position. When our man tries to break in, we'll nab him. Thanks a million, professor. This has helped a lot."

"Wait! I need to go with you."

Daniel cocked his head. "No, you don't."

"We need to find the clue to the cryptex."

"No, we need to bag the bad guy," Daniel explained. This happened sometimes, an informant getting overexcited and thinking they were a bigger part of the investigation than they really were.

"Look, if the killer figured out one of the clues is in the de Lacy collection, then someone else might. We need to find it before that information causes a crime in the future."

Good point. This woman had a quick mind. Daniel smiled. "All right, professor, you win. Just tell me which artifact it's in and I'll check it out. Well, some museum curator will check it out. I'm sure they won't let me touch anything."

Professor Laurent made a face. "I'm not sure which artifact it's in. I need to take a look at them. While I'm fairly familiar with the de Lacy collection, I've never seen them up close. Most of the pieces have never been on display before."

Daniel hesitated, then said, "All right. We'll meet at the museum right after closing. It will still be light then and the killer only strikes late at night. But you only get fifteen minutes." The professor opened her mouth to object, but Daniel rolled right over her. "We can't run the risk that the killer is watching and might spot you, so you go in, check the place out, tip us off to which artifact to keep an eye on, and then you leave. All right?"

"But—"

"All *right*?"

Professor Laurent did not look happy. Nevertheless, she mumbled, "All right."

"Good," Daniel said in a tone that indicated the conversation was over. "We'll meet ten minutes after closing time. The visitors should have cleared out by then. Thank you, professor, this has been a great help."

He meant it. Maybe they could bag the bad guy this very night, and he could get back to his real work.

Finger Man was still out there, hunting young male athletes, and he was past due for his next killing.

CHAPTER FIVE

The Chosen One drove with the window open, breathing in the rich smells of the New England forest. His eyes felt heavy and gritty from lack of sleep. His gut protested at the several cups of coffee he had downed during his brief rest stops as he drove in a winding route. His legs and lower back felt stiff from driving for so many hours. His neck was beginning to ache too.

And yet he felt content. He was doing the Lord's work.

And what a place to do it in! Ever since leaving the Glencairn Museum with the Gorizia dodecahedron, the Chosen One had spent the last two days driving around some of the oldest churches of the land. He had headed through eastern Pennsylvania, then north and east to cut through the southern Hudson Valley before moving due east into Connecticut and then north into Massachusetts. Avoiding the highways, he took the winding two-lane county roads through villages and isolated farmland.

He stopped only for gas, or to sit and pray in the old colonial churches of the seventeenth and early eighteenth centuries, sacred relics of a time when this had been a Godly land.

While time was of the essence in the great work he had been commanded to do, his meandering path was necessary. First, it calmed him. The old sacred places always calmed him, cleared his mind and strengthened his faith. He knew he was a weak vessel. After the last two sacrifices he needed to bolster his will, and nowhere did he feel closer to God than in some fine old wooden building whose walls had echoed with prayers for centuries.

His large detour served a worldly purpose as well. At his stops at gas stations, he would make sure to park where his license plate was clearly visible to the camera, and he would go inside to make some small purchase or other, where in the brightly lit interior his face would be recognizable on the camera.

There were those who would stop him, those who saw his liberation of the ancient secrets as theft, and his sacrifices as murder.

Unwitting tools of Satan. He must fool them all.

So he drove and prayed, prayed and drove. He was a Godly man, a pure man. All his impurity had been washed away through prayer, meditation, and shedding the blood of the unbelievers.

And once he had been purified, he had been rewarded with a revelation.

The sun dipped down behind the trees, twinkling through the thick foliage. With night coming on, his body betrayed him. He let out a wide yawn.

He slammed his fist into his forehead three times.

The weakness of the flesh! After all his efforts, his flesh remained weak!

The throbbing pain in his forehead kept him awake and alert as he drove on. A sign told him Washington, D.C., was still 150 miles down the road. Once he made it, he'd find a motel. Too late in the evening to get started this night. These things took preparation. Thought. One should not rush the work of the Lord.

For to fail would lead to damnation.

So he wouldn't break in tonight. He'd find a motel, sleep the sleep of the just, and tomorrow he'd continue on to the museum. He'd walk through the building when it was open to get a better look at it and break in once it had closed for the night.

In the rapidly dimming light of dusk, he spotted a hitchhiker up ahead, walking along the verge close to the line of trees. He'd seen many on his marathon multi-state journey and had passed by them all. Something about this one made him look twice.

The hitchhiker looked significantly older than the driver's forty years. Maybe in his fifties or sixties. Wiry and bent, with a salt and pepper beard reaching halfway to his stomach, he carried a large backpack as he walked down the side of the highway with his thumb extended.

On the back of the backpack was painted a large white cross. That was what had caught the Chosen One's attention. That and the fact that they were far from any town.

"A Godly man in the wilderness," the Chosen One said to himself, his voice coming out hoarse.

He slowed as he passed the hitchhiker and pulled off on the shoulder. In his sideview mirror he saw the man grin and trot up to him.

"Where are you going?" the Chosen One croaked.

"D.C."

"The Lord has smiled on you. So am I. Throw your pack over the seat into the back. Just be careful not to hit the dummy."

The hitchhiker knelt on the passenger seat and pushed his backpack over into the back, which was half filled with toolboxes and more than a hundred books stored neatly in milk crates. In a large, padded box, open at the top, lay a remarkably realistic three-foot-high dummy. It looked like a young boy, with shorts and a little button-down shirt, a happy smile, wide blue eyes, and a cowlick on his painted blonde hair.

Only its skin looked unreal. It was gold.

The hitchhiker stared at it a moment before closing the door and buckling up.

The driver hit the accelerator and sped down the two-lane road. No cars were in sight.

"Thanks for picking me up. With it getting dark I was praying I wouldn't have to spend the night in the woods."

"You a Godly man?" the driver asked in his croaking voice.

"Yes, I am. Saved at a service at Yahweh Evangelical Church in Carson City, Nevada, thirty years ago. Been on the straight and narrow ever since."

"Hallelujah."

The driver picked up speed. They were a bit southeast of Allentown, passing through state game lands. No houses here, nor farmland. A sign gave directions for Lake Nockamixon State Park.

"When were you saved?" the hitchhiker asked.

"Fifteen years ago. I wasted my life before then. God granted me the chance to turn my life around after he saved me from dying of an overdose."

The hitchhiker made a face. "I used to dabble in that stuff before I saw the light."

"I was in it pretty badly. Smoking heroin."

The hitchhiker looked at him. "I thought people injected heroin."

"Most people do. I didn't like needles. I was afraid of blood back then. So I smoked it. It ruined my voice."

"Sorry to hear that."

"It's all right." The driver made a ghost of a smile. His muscles, unused to the expression, felt stiff. "I have someone else to speak for me."

A chirpy child's voice came from the back of the van.

"Praise the Lord. When I grow up, I'm going to be a soldier for Christ."

The hitchhiker looked over his shoulder, and not seeing anyone back there, he looked at the dummy and then back at the driver, grinning.

"I was about to ask if that was a ventriloquist dummy. That was amazing. How did your voice come out so clear?"

"One of the Lord's many miracles," the driver said in his own hoarse whisper, "When I throw my voice it comes out as clear and pure as when I was a boy."

"You do shows?"

"Yes, I offer my services to Sunday schools all over the land. The children love that little dummy."

The ventriloquist's dummy started to sing.

"Jesus loves me this I know, because the Bible tells me so."

The hitchhiker laughed. "We used to sing that in Bible camp. I wish I had embraced the Lord then instead of straying from the path."

"Bible camp," the Chosen One grumbled. "It's no wonder you strayed if you went to one of those pits of sin."

The hitchhiker gave him a curious look. "Pits of sin?"

"Pits of vice and sin!"

"Easy, brother. I don't know what Bible camp you went to, but my—"

"A nest of vipers! Satan's kindergarten!" the driver shouted so loudly his voice cracked. He rubbed his throat and winced.

Don't be shy, kid. Where in Scripture does it say we can't do this? And remember, the Bible says you must obey your elders.

The hitchhiker raised his hands. "Whoa! Whoa! No need to get upset."

"The Lord will wreak his vengeance. I am only a weak vessel, submitting to His will," the driver said, his voice a gravelly whisper.

The hitchhiker stiffened and looked out the window.

They drove in silence for a couple of minutes, the darkness gathering over the land. The headlights shone on an empty highway.

Softly, the ventriloquist dummy began to sing, its pure voice lilting from the back of the van.

"Sinners all burn in hell,
And the Lord smiles at the smell,
The righteous slay the unbelievers,

And tear the throats of deceivers."

The hitchhiker cleared his throat. "You know, I think I want to camp for the night. You see, um, I forgot I had promised to meet up with someone back in East Brunswick. So, I'll just camp and hitch a ride going the other direction tomorrow morning. Sure is nice to meet you, though. Now if you could just let me off here, that would be fine, and God bless you."

The driver slumped his shoulders. Another weak will. Another half Christian.

A sign for a scenic view appeared in the headlights.

"I'll drop you off at the vista point. That way it will be easier to get a ride in early morning when people stop to see the view."

"That would be real Christian of you," the hitchhiker said in a tight voice.

He took off his seat belt, turned in his seat, and pulled his backpack over the seat. Just as he did so, two things happened: an approaching car with its high beams on sped up behind them, shining light through the windows of the van's rear doors and illuminating the back; at the same moment, the hitchhiker yanked his pack up and accidentally knocked over a toolbox. It fell open, and wire cutters and a large knife fell out. Stains on the blade could just be made out in the dim light.

Stiffly, the hitchhiker sat down, pretending he didn't notice.

But the Chosen One noticed.

He slowed, and as the overtaking vehicle passed and the pull-off came into view, he turned onto it. He stopped in a small parking lot with a descriptive sign looking out over a small, forested valley, half hidden in the dark.

"This will be fine right here," the hitchhiker said.

"I'll get you a bit away from the highway, so the noise doesn't disturb your sleep."

"That's all right. I can walk."

The hitchhiker's voice had an edge to it now. His hand rested on the door latch, even though they were still moving. The headlights revealed a narrow Park Service road of cracked concrete leading out of the parking lot and down into the valley. Here and there tufts of grass pushed out from the asphalt.

"I can walk from here," the hitchhiker repeated.

The driver didn't seem to hear him or didn't care. Instead of responding to his statement, he said instead,

"For the rare seeker, the one who keeps to the true path, there is a way to know God better than anyone other than the Apostles themselves. There is a lock, but before one can open the lock one must find it, and to find it one must assemble the key. That will both tell you the location of the lock and give you the means by which to open it. And when the right man opens it, all will be revealed, and the man so blessed will be like one of the Apostles."

The driver coughed and rubbed his throat. He was unaccustomed to talking so much with his own voice. When he threw his voice into Little Peter, it didn't hurt his throat. Only when he spoke for himself did his sinful old habit cause him pain.

He licked his lips, swallowed, and continued as he drove slowly down the Park Service road and the hitchhiker fidgeted beside him.

"I have been searching for the key for many years. Its pieces have been scattered and hidden. It is a difficult path, and few stay on it for long. I've met many who try and quickly fail. Godless fools, mostly. I know of only one other seeker who is truly committed. She may be Godless too. I don't know. I hope not. I have learned so much from her. Someday I'll meet her. If she is Godless, I will correct her. If she is Godly, I will make her my wife. She will bear me many children I will put on the right path. Together as a family we will wash this sinful land clean the only way sin can be cleaned from the land."

From the back, Little Peter said, "The streets will run red with the blood of the unbelievers."

The driver slowed the van and stopped.

"Thanks, brother!" the hitchhiker said, already jumping out. "This will be just fine."

The hitchhiker took off running, struggling to put on his pack. Calmly the Chosen One put the van in park, switched off his headlights, looked around for the lights of any approaching vehicle and, seeing none, reached in the back and retrieved the knife.

He did not rush. The hitchhiker was loaded down with a pack and had nowhere to hide. Plus, as an instrument of God's will, there was no chance he would not manage to chase down his quarry.

In the last dim light of dusk, the driver could just make out the hitchhiker. He had left the road and tried to cut across the woods, only to trip in the gloom and fall. Now he struggled to get up. It looked like he had hurt his ankle.

The driver walked toward him, hand gripping the knife.

"Stay away from me!" the hitchhiker cried, shucking off his backpack and managing to get up. He turned and hobbled off. The Chosen One increased his pace, narrowing the space between them. But he did not run. He did not need to. God had hurt this false Christian, this devil in disguise who might go to the police, those Pharisees who pervert the words of the Lord.

The Chosen One's heavy boots crushed the undergrowth and gave him firm footing on the wet, uneven ground. The hitchhiker, trying to hurry in worn old sneakers, kept slipping or getting caught up, slowing him further.

"What do you want!" the hitchhiker pleaded.

"To open the lock," the driver replied. "To reveal God's hidden secrets and purify the world. But I do not have to wait to purify the world. I can start purifying it right now."

The hitchhiker's eyes bugged in terror. He picked up a rock and threw it. The driver dodged it easily. As he bent to pick up another, the Chosen One rushed him.

"Please!"

The hitchhiker grabbed the Chosen One's knife arm, but with his free arm the Chosen One gave him a powerful punch that knocked him flat. The Chosen One grabbed him by his hair and pulled him up, putting the keen edge of the knife to his throat.

"No," the hitchhiker whispered. "You're a Godly man. I can see that. You're a good man. Think. Would God want this? This is not God's way."

The driver snorted. "You don't know God's way. So few people do."

He cut deep into the hitchhiker's throat, the blood gushing onto the damp forest soil.

"Thy will be done," the Chosen One intoned.

As the man flailed and choked on his own blood, the Chosen One began to gather stones and brush to pile on top of him. A low ditch and some bushes provided cover to hide the backpack.

The body and backpack would not remain hidden forever. Sooner or later, the Devil would lead someone to them. But he did not have time to bury it properly. He had to hurry on to the capital of this accursed nation. He prayed God would grant him enough time to do His work.

Once he had hidden everything as well as time allowed, and cleaned the knife on some leaves, he walked back to the van, feeling at peace, his mind clear. The Lord had sent this false Christian into his path as a sign. The Lord wanted to test his fortitude. He had been tired, worn down, needing his little road trip around the old churches in order to buck up his spirit.

What he really needed was greater faith in God's master plan.

Where once he had felt weary, now every nerve sang with energy. His hooded, gritty eyes now sparkled. The stiffness of hours of driving had vanished. As he climbed into the van, he felt like he could drive all the way to California that very night and kill every sinner in the state.

Leaving the door open so the light remained on, he quickly checked that no blood had gotten onto his overalls. He did not see any. He was getting good at slaughtering the unrighteous without leaving traces. Having that knife in the top of a toolbox, a toolbox he had forgotten to latch, that was a slipup.

Slipups were unacceptable.

He smacked his forehead with his fist three times.

"A weak vessel," he shouted. "I am a weak vessel!"

He gripped the wheel, his heart pounding fast. The calm he usually felt after sending a sinner to Hell was tinged with the realization that he had stumbled, made mistakes. God did not accept mistakes.

"I will try to do better, my Lord," he whispered.

Glancing around to make sure no vehicles were close by, he made a three-point turn on the service road, turned on his headlights, and headed back to the county road.

His mood began to calm. It would be all right. While the Lord knew he was frail, He also knew he was determined. The Chosen One would do anything for the Lord.

Only a little more time until D.C. Only a little more time and he would have another piece of the key.

And in order to thank the Lord, he would sacrifice another sinner.

From the back of the van, Little Peter began to sing in a sweet, high voice.

"Jesus loves me, this I know, because the Bible tells me so."

CHAPTER SIX

At six in the evening, Remi locked up her office, already exhausted even though the worst part of the day still lay ahead of her. The revelations about someone hunting the cryptex, someone who obviously knew things she didn't, had put her in an almost trancelike state, thinking and rethinking the possibilities.

Now she had to go to The Twenty-First Century Museum of Culture in Washington, D.C., where she felt sure the serial killer would strike next.

Remi trembled as she locked her office and checked for the third time that her can of pepper spray was in the inside pocket of her purse where she could get at it quickly.

While she felt afraid, she also felt strangely exhilarated. Someone was hunting for the cryptex, someone who might have a chance of actually finding it.

They had to capture him. She needed to talk with this man. Find out what he knew, find out what his sources were.

Passing down a hallway crowded with chattering students—buoyant that the last class of the day had just let out—she headed for the nearest exit, feeling a bit left out. She could have never walked this far on the Sorbonne campus without being stopped at least once by some eager student asking a question. She wrote about fascinating topics—medieval cryptography, magical grimoires, secret societies—and there was always some wide-eyed young person wanting to know more.

At Georgetown, though, it seemed like people had no sense of curiosity. Everyone was too busy posting about themselves online to care about the mysteries of the past.

At least here she got more funding for travel and research materials.

And something more …

As she went out the double doors into the fresh evening air and descended a flight of marble steps, she did find someone waiting for her—Dr. Cyril Mullen, head of the history department. She stopped in surprise. Showing up unannounced was one of his more annoying traits. Then he flashed her his winning grin. Her heart warmed and she felt her face flush like a schoolgirl's.

They had met at a conference three years before and had felt an immediate and mutual attraction. At fifty he was twelve years her senior but still an imposing figure with salt-and-pepper hair swept back over a broad forehead and an athletic body, being as good on the racquetball court as he was in bed. He was also a first-rate historian specializing in nineteenth century American diplomacy. Remi had found it best to pick lovers who studied very different subjects. Less of a sense of competition that way.

The last time she had dated a medievalist, the man practically had a fit when she got a book deal before he did.

"How did your day go?" Cyril asked, giving her a professional smile. Only a twinkle in his gray eyes gave away his real feelings. They had to keep it professional in public.

"Oh God, you wouldn't believe what happened," she said.

Cyril fell in beside her as they walked.

"You alight?" he asked, concern stamped on his face.

Remi shook her head.

"Still up for dinner tonight?" he asked in a low voice, as if it was a top-secret meeting. Remi felt a trace of irritation. Didn't she just tell him she wasn't doing well? As if sensing his blunder, Cyril went on, "We can go right now and get a drink first. You can tell me all about it."

Remi stopped short raised her face to the sky. "Oh, I'm sorry, I completely forgot about dinner. The FBI came to visit me today."

"What?"

"You know the break-in at the Cloisters?"

"Yeah, I was the one who told you about it."

"Oh, that's right. Well, there's been another break-in at the Glencairn Museum. It looks like the killer is after the lost clues to the cryptex."

Cyril's face took on a dubious expression. While he didn't mock her pursuit of the cryptex like some of her colleagues at the Sorbonne, once or twice he'd said that she was better off sticking to her "more serious subjects."

It was a sore point between them, one they had made an unspoken agreement not to bring up.

And now she had broken that agreement.

“How can you know he’s after that thing?” Cyril said.

Remi started walking again, Cyril beside her.

“In both cases he broke hollow objects in order to retrieve something inside. In the case of the Glencairn Museum, it was a plaster bust made just at the right time when the secret society was hiding the clues. There were traces of copper stains inside.”

Cyril raised an eyebrow. “That Roman artifact?”

“That’s what I’m thinking.”

Remi was surprised Cyril remembered the details of her studies. Maybe he took them more seriously than she realized?

That was cleared up with his next statement.

“I suppose it doesn’t matter if it isn’t real if the killer thinks it is.”

“It is real,” Remi snapped. “The hollow bust proves it.”

“Stains on the inside of a bit of plaster. Come on, Remi.”

They fell silent for a moment.

A shadow passed over Cyril’s face. They stopped in the middle of the sidewalk, making an undergraduate couple holding hands behind them temporarily let go of each other as they passed around them, before closing up and taking each other’s hands again.

“So are we still going to dinner?” Cyril asked.

How can you think of dinner when a killer is hunting down my research subject!

As irritated as she was, she didn’t say that. Instead, she said, “I have to go to that new museum on the south side with the FBI agent. I need to meet him there right now.”

“I suppose you have no choice,” Cyril grumbled again. He had been grumbling a lot lately.

“I really must go. Sorry about dinner.” She turned to leave.

“All right, you go play cops and robbers.” He wagged a finger at her. “But I’m monopolizing your time tomorrow night.”

Remi smiled. “All right.”

She continued across Georgetown’s leafy and busy campus, passing flirting undergraduates and preoccupied professors. She felt a bit preoccupied herself.

The wasn’t the first time Cyril had surprised her somewhere, asked her to have a coffee or go for a walk, and her automatic reaction had been to make up an excuse why she couldn’t.

This was the first time she actually had a valid excuse.

Remi didn't understand why she did that. She had come to Georgetown for him, and he knew that. The prestigious visiting lecturer status and sizeable research grant were simply icing on an already tasty cake.

And yet, she felt there was something a bit off about her relationship with Cyril. Something she couldn't quite put her finger on. When they had a plan and stuck to it, she felt entirely at ease. Tonight, for example, would have been wonderful. She just knew it. But his unexpected appearance and request for her time before the hour they had set made her feel trapped. Hunted, almost.

Things were moving too fast. Far too fast.

She reached her car and got inside, putting her relationship troubles aside. She had more important things to think about tonight.

She might finally discover the truth about her lifelong obsession.

* * *

Daniel Walker's microwave pinged. He opened it and pulled out a steaming burrito on a plate. He bathed the burrito in habanero sauce and plunked it down on the kitchen table of the small, one-bedroom apartment he'd moved to until he could patch things up with his wife Veronica.

He hoped that would be soon. He missed living in a house instead of a crappy apartment, and he missed eating her home cooking instead of frozen microwave burritos.

Maybe once I bust this museum killer I can get back on track with my career. Then I'll bust Finger Man and I can ask for some time off. Veronica would like that.

But what about the Southwest Strangler? No, take some time off, dumbass, or you'll lose her.

Finger Man. I wonder what's going on with Finger Man. I haven't checked in for twelve hours.

As he dug into his burrito, he pulled out his phone and called his partner, Agent Nomellini.

Ex-partner, he reminded himself. *At least for the moment.*

She picked up on the third ring.

Agent Nomellini's familiar Brooklyn accent came over the line. "Hey, Danny boy."

"Yo, Carmella. What's up?"

"Cooking up some rigatoni for the husband and the hellions."

Daniel could hear the hellions in the background, twin seven-year-old boys screaming as they tore through the house thwacking each other with their favorite toys—a pair of foam light sabers. Actually, they were little sweethearts. They cuddled up to "Uncle Danny" anytime he came over and squealed with joy when he spun them around. But there was no way you could get a pair of seven-year-olds to either sit still or be quiet. It was biologically impossible.

"Sounds fun," Daniel said, feeling a tug of loneliness. He wanted kids. Veronica didn't want kids "with someone who cared more about serial killers than his family." It was one of their points of tension. One among a thousand.

"How's the new Antiquities Division?" Agent Nomellini asked.

"Ugh. Weird. I don't feel like explaining. But I got a good civilian contact that's helping me track down the perp. Turns out the guy might hit a place in D.C. next. With any luck we'll ambush him tonight and I'll be back on the Finger Man case tomorrow."

"You think they'll let you go?" His ex-partner sounded hopeful.

"God, I hope so. How's the case going?"

"Working on all the leads. That info you got from the drug dealer helped."

"So flushing his head down the toilet was worth it?" Daniel asked with a smile.

"It would have been worth it even if he didn't know anything."

Daniel laughed. At least someone on the force understood him.

"How's Agent Dunning working out?" he asked.

"Ugh. The less said about that moron the better."

A child's voice cut in. "Mom, who are you talking to?"

"Uncle Danny."

"Cool! Is he coming over for dinner?"

"No. Uncle Danny has to work tonight."

"Uncle Danny works too hard. You said so."

Daniel rolled his eyes. Even the kids had it out for him.

"Go play."

"Tell Uncle Danny you don't want him working so hard. Tell him he needs a life."

"Go play! Sorry about that, Daniel."

Daniel forced himself to laugh. "No problem. I've heard it before." The doorbell rang. "Look, I got to go. Keep me updated, all right?"

"Sure thing. You eating OK?"

Daniel glanced at his microwave burrito. "Yeah, I'm mixing up a Caesar salad as we speak."

"OK. Keep you posted."

Daniel hung up. The doorbell rang again.

"I'm coming, I'm coming," he muttered, crossing his narrow living room and opening the door, keeping the chain in place. Years of hunting heartless killers had made him cautious.

A nondescript man in his thirties wearing a Yankees cap said, "Mr. Daniel Walker?"

"Yes."

He pushed an envelope through the crack in the door. "You have been served."

The man walked away. Daniel closed the door and tore open the envelope.

"Shit," he muttered. Inside were the divorce papers, and a note:

"This is the third time I've sent these. I'm trying to be nice. My lawyer tells me I can do this with or without your cooperation. Sign these. Now."

Daniel threw the papers on the floor and went back to his burrito.

Taking a bite of his burrito, he hiccupped from the generous dollop of habanero sauce.

What the hell happened? They'd been married for nearly eight years and at the beginning it was great. Lots of nights out with friends, lots of nights tumbling in bed. Walks. Movies. They'd both been dedicated to work—him with his investigative work, her climbing the ladder at IBM—but they accepted that about each other. Their careers had been a source of mutual respect.

But somewhere along the line things changed. Veronica hit a glass ceiling. For a while she fought it, and when she couldn't rise any further, and couldn't find a more enticing job elsewhere, she began to look outward. While she still worked hard, now her focus had turned to things other than career. Yoga. A book club. Volunteering at an adult literacy program. Hikes in Virginia's lush woodland.

Daniel participated in none of these things. Just as her world expanded, his grew ever more narrow. He got assigned to the Behavioral Analysis Unit, where he tracked down serial killers. His first bust, just three months into the job, got him hooked. A wedding photographer who developed an obsession with some of the brides he photographed. The guy convinced himself they had married the wrong person and they needed to be saved by their dream man—him. When he kidnapped them and found the poor women weren't over the moon with love, he cut them into little pieces and moved on to his next obsession.

Daniel had figured out who it was, and when the SWAT team busted through his door, they found him sharpening his knives, preparing to kill his latest failed love.

Saving a life got him seriously addicted. He realized that the harder he worked, the more lives he'd save. The job became a rabbit hole into which he quickly got lost.

Veronica was right. So was Agent Nomellini. Hell, even her kids could see it. Daniel had become a workaholic, and workaholics made for really boring company.

But what else could he do, when taking a vacation might lead to somebody's preventable death? He was good at what he did. The best. It was easy for Veronica to ease back from her job. If she screwed up a quarterly report, no one would get dismembered and put in garbage bags.

Despite that, he couldn't get mad at her. Not really. He could see it from her side. The missed dinners. The working weekends. No woman wanted that.

Plus, the kid thing. She wanted kids but not with him. He wanted kids but couldn't have them. He might have been an expert marksman on the firing range, but in bed he shot blanks.

Daniel slammed a fist on the table. There had to be some way. Some compromise. Maybe he could carve out two nights a week for her that would be sacred, no matter what was going on in the case. Agent Nomellini could take up the slack. She'd volunteered several times when Daniel had talked about his and Veronica's troubles. If only Veronica would give him a second chance.

Daniel finished his burrito, belched, and looked at his watch. Damn, time to hit the road. He had to meet that professor at The Twenty-First Century Museum of Culture in less than an hour. She was going to take a look at the collection and try to figure out what object would be the target of this psycho. If he could bag this guy in the next couple of days, maybe he could get back to his regular job at the Behavioral Analysis Unit. Maybe then he could get some stability back in his career and hash things out with Veronica.

But as he strapped on his holster and put on his jacket, he wasn't even thinking about Veronica. He stepped over the discarded divorce papers still lying on the floor and headed out into the dusk, his mind filled with plans for catching the Cryptex Killer.

CHAPTER SEVEN

Remi pulled into the parking lot, hands sweating as she gripped the steering wheel. This was the closest she had ever come to her life's goal. Could one of the keys to the cryptex really be inside this building?

The Twenty-First Century Museum of Culture stood on the edges of Washington, D.C.'s tourist and governmental center in an older commercial district of brick buildings built a hundred years before. Just to the south, the neighborhood grew worse and worse. One didn't have to drive far to get to the slums.

Remi had never been here. She'd been warned about the dangers of a lone woman coming to this neighborhood. Cyril had never suggested a trip to the city's newest museum.

The reason a city already rich with cultural institutions, including the world-famous Smithsonian, got a museum close to the bad side of town was thanks to Carter Green, the country's first African American dot com billionaire. Making his initial millions investing in crypto currency when everyone else was still laughing it off as a geeky fad, he funneled those profits into black-friendly online news outlets, video streaming sites, and special interest shops. He'd even set up an online vendor called Serengeti to rival Amazon.

Carter Green had been born a few blocks to the south, and had decided to lift up the area by building his own private museum and stuffing it with one of the world's biggest private collections of fine art.

Only a couple of other cars were in the parking lot. For a moment she felt nervous. The streets in this mostly commercial district were quiet, and the only place she saw open was a hair salon across the street, which made her feel a little better, and a bar a few doors down, which made her feel worse.

She stepped out of her car, her hand unzipping her purse in case she needed to grab her pepper spray.

The museum was housed in a four-story reused office building from the 1950s, facing a broad street and hemmed in by buildings on three other sides. Flanking the stairs up to the front door were a pair of Egyptian sphinxes.

They looked real. Remi wondered how much Carter Green had paid for them.

She spotted Agent Walker standing at the foot of the stairs leading up to the museum's heavy black double doors and let out a breath of relief.

Remi waved to the FBI agent and hurried over.

"Thanks for coming," Agent Walker said. "The local PD is sending a couple of plainclothes officers to help out. They're late."

Remi blinked. "PD?"

Agent Walker smiled. "Police department. Don't you watch television?"

"No."

He cocked his head and gave her a dubious look. "Not even the History Channel?"

"Ancient aliens? Nazi astrologers? No, thank you."

"When all this is said and done maybe you can do a documentary for them about the cryptex."

"They already offered. I said no."

I get laughed at enough at work. I don't need that from the general public too.

They turned to ascend the stairs.

A security guard stood at the open doors waiting for them. His was a rake-thin man who looked in his sixties. His light blue uniform hung loosely on him, and his cap was all wrinkled, as if he had sat on it by accident.

Agent Walker let out a derisive snort. "A nightstick and a can of pepper spray. I feel safer already."

"I'm sure he'll do his best."

"Their best wasn't good enough in the last two places. We're going to have to do our best to keep this jackass alive."

Remi thought the FBI agent was being unkind but, considering what happened to the last two security guards, she could understand him being a bit edgy.

They ascended the stairs. The man came up to them with an arthritic gait.

"You must be Agent Walker. I'm Edgar Brown, head of security for the museum."

Remi watched as the FBI agent put on a poker face and shook his hand.

"Good to meet you, Edgar. This is my civilian colleague Dr. Remi Laurent. I presume the museum management already briefed you on the phone, so how about you take us around and show us your security arrangements."

"All right. Let's look at the outside, and then I'll take you in. My men are locking up. The last visitors only left half an hour ago."

Remi bit her lip, her heart fluttering in her chest. From what Agent Walker had told her, the last two break-ins happened in the dead of night. Still, just knowing the museum was closed and was the next target made it feel like the killer was watching her.

Edgar led them slowly around the grounds. While Remi was hardly an expert in security matters, it didn't look terribly safe. There were alleys on two sides, making convenient hiding places. Because of the style of brickwork, climbing to a window would be easy. While the ground floor windows had bars, the upper story windows did not. The security guard pointed out that CCTV cameras covered all the approaches, and the building was fitted with the "latest security system."

The back had a wider alley, really a narrow access road with a loading dock. The metal shutters were down, and a heavy padlock sealed it. Facing it was the back of another building that faced the adjoining street. An identical loading dock, also closed, was all there was to see except for a bit of scattered trash.

Edgar led them up back to the front yard, where the parking lot and a small lawn was all there was to see. They went up the steps to the front entrance, a large pair of heavy wooden doors. Two younger security guards waited outside, one a pimply faced white kid who couldn't have been more than nineteen, the other an African American who looked only slightly older but who already sported a belly.

"So where are your other men?" Agent Walker asked.

"This is it," Edgar replied.

"But the museum said it was increasing its security," Remi said.

"They did. Usually it's just one of us."

"How can you monitor the security cameras and do rounds when there's only one of you?"

The security guard shrugged. "Ask the budget director. Most museums are like this."

Agent Walker muttered something Remi didn't catch.

A car pulled into the parking lot and two bulky men got out.

"The cavalry has arrived," Remi whispered to Agent Walker, using one of the few American phrases she knew. The FBI man gave her a sly wink, making her smile.

The two men who came up the stairs might have been wearing civilian clothes—slacks and polo shirts—but Remi could tell they were police from a mile off. They had the buzz cuts and moustaches that seemed to be regulation among American police officers. At least they weren't obese, another all too common feature of American law enforcement, and the population in general.

One officer had brown hair, the other had blonde hair. Otherwise, they looked very much alike.

The blonde spoke. "I'm Officer Smith. This is Officer Smith. No relation."

"Glad to have you on board," Agent Walker said as everyone shook hands and introduced themselves.

"Sorry we couldn't bring in more people," the blonde Officer Smith said. "Just a few blocks south of here the Bloods and Crips have decided to blast away at each other over a few crappy street corners. Two dead and five in the hospital just in the past week. Every available man is down there right now. It's actually our day off."

"Well, thanks for coming in," Remi said.

"No problem, professor. Sure beats running around the warzone."

Agent Walker cut in. "Mr. Brown has just shown us the grounds. Now he's going to show us the interior."

They passed through the main entrance and into a large circular foyer. A huge photograph of Carter Green, smiling in his Armani suit, rose ten feet up one wall. A trim man in his forties with an erect posture, Green looked off to the distance, his gaze slightly upward as if looking out at the stars. Indeed, Remi had read he was contemplating getting into the private space race many of his peers had started a few years before.

In the center of the foyer stood an ancient Egyptian statue of Horus, one foot planted in front of the other, arms stiff at his sides. The ceiling was open to two of the upper stories, with marble banisters running around.

"Mr. Green is a big fan of ancient Egypt," Edgar said. "The whole ground floor is dedicated to Egypt and other African civilizations."

"I'm down with Carter Green," the brown-haired Officer Smith said. "I bought a tablet on Serengeti last week."

Remi rolled her eyes. He sounded like he wanted a medal.

"A fine citizen," the blonde Officer Smith said. "Wish more took his example."

Remi and Agent Walker exchanged looks. Remi was beginning to understand why they hadn't been put on gang duty.

Edgar led them through the half-lit museum as Remi's gaze passed appreciatively over a small but choice collection of Egyptian and sub-Saharan African art. They went up some service stairs to the second floor, devoted to the Classical civilizations, Remi feeling increasingly impatient until they got to the third floor where the museum's medieval collection was held, passing along darkened display cases of swords and icons to a wing devoted to temporary exhibitions.

"We've locked this up tight," Edgar said proudly. "You mentioned your man is good at disabling security systems, so we added a low-tech feature."

He motioned to the door, leading to the wing, which had a thick chain around the heavy brass handles. The chain was secured by a large padlock.

"He can pick locks too," Agent Walker said.

Edgar flushed.

"Well, we got security cameras. Let me show you the camera room."

They headed up to the fourth floor, devoted to 20th century art, and to a small room near the back with a desk, a couple of chairs, and a bank of security cameras.

"I guess this is home for the night," Remi said and sighed.

Agent Walker gave her a concerned look. "What? You're not staying here. We're going to go down to the special exhibition, you're going to give us an idea of the item he might want, and then you're going home."

Despite her nervousness, Remi shook her head. "It's better if I'm here. I might be able to give you some insight into what he might do. I may even be able to talk him down."

"Talk him down?"

"He must know about me. Anyone who studies the cryptex does. Maybe I can reason with him."

"More likely he'll start swinging with that knife of his," the FBI agent said.

Remi felt a prickle of fear.

"Don't worry. I'll leave the fighting to you," she said with more confidence than she felt.

Agent Walker paused. Remi got the impression that he wanted her here. Remi smiled. It felt good to be taken seriously. She didn't get enough of that. He glanced at the other men in the room and then said,

"I can't allow you to do that. It would be unethical for us to endanger a civilian."

Remi raised her hands in protest. "I'm going to be with three police officers."

"Three officers who have to guard a large building from a very determined and cunning killer," Agent Walker said.

"We appreciate your enthusiasm, ma'am," the blonde Officer Smith said, "but the three of us are going to busy enough trying to collar the perp. We won't be able to provide you adequate protection."

No one mentioned or even thought of the three security guards.

"Let's go take a look at the special exhibition and then I'll see you to your car," Agent Walker said. "I'll call you if anything comes up."

Irritation tinged her worry.

I'm supposed to sit at home while all the big, tough men face an enemy they don't even understand? We'll see about that.

While the pot-bellied security guard stayed in the camera room and the pimply-faced one went on his rounds, Edgar led the rest down to the temporary exhibitions gallery. In front of the padlocked doors hung a sign that read, "Medieval Treasures of the Cluny Museum, Paris."

"So you're sure our guy is going to break into this show?" the blonde Officer Smith asked her.

"Quite sure," Remi answered, barely even registering his question.

"Where?" Edgar asked as he took off the padlock and yanked away the chain with a loud rattle.

"Give me a minute and I'll tell you," she answered, passing through the doors before the security guard had fully opened them.

She paused just inside the doorway as Edgar turned on the lights to reveal various display cases of gold reliquaries, delicate ivory tryptics, and other masterpieces of medieval art.

"So one of these works of art holds a clue to unlocking this cryptex thing," the blonde Officer Smith said.

"Yes," Remi said, slowly stepping into the exhibition space, her eyes feasting on the beautiful displays of fine art, and the promise of knowledge they contained.

"So which artifact is it?" the police officer asked.

Remi let out an embarrassed shrug. "I haven't been able to discover that. I didn't know about the bust at the Glencairn museum or the figurine at the Cloisters either. The killer seems to have discovered a source of information I missed."

"Is that how he found out about this, um, cabal of old millionaires you mentioned?"

Remi winced. "He probably found out about that from the latest paper I published."

Edgar let out a grunt, then asked, "Why didn't he hit the exhibition earlier? It's been on for nearly two months."

"I don't know. I think he's just discovered the information," Remi said.

"Well, he's going to have to make his play soon, we're only showing this stuff for another week," Edgar said.

Remi nodded as she walked between the display cases. Yes, it was now or never. He might be out in the streets right now, hiding in the shadows and checking out the building.

Someone who knew something about the cryptex she didn't.

She had to meet him, no matter what the risk.

So in what artifact had de Lacy hidden his piece of the puzzle? She had studied images of his collection time and again and could pick out each of the artifacts amid the wealth of other items on display.

Then she came to case containing a fourteenth century icon, and it hit her.

Like a thunderbolt, it hit her.

"*Mon Dieu,*" she whispered. "There it is."

CHAPTER EIGHT

"Here, right here!" the professor cried. "Of course! Why hadn't I thought of it before?"

Daniel hurried over to where Professor Laurent stood in front of an icon of John the Baptist standing on the shore of the River Jordan, baptizing Jesus. The figures were a dark brown against a gold background, a style common to the Byzantine era, but the figures were livelier, more realistic, in the Italian style.

Long time since I studied this stuff, Daniel thought. *Amazing I still remember any of it.*

"You sure this is the right one?" the FBI agent asked. The police officers and Edgar came over.

The professor was grinning ear to ear, shaking with excitement.

"I'm positive. De Lacy was a devout Catholic, and he was especially interested in the story of the Baptism of Jesus. He got into trouble with the Church for writing a pamphlet calling for adult baptism. He said that if Jesus got baptized as an adult, so should regular people, and that infant baptism was an act of tradition rather than true faith."

"That's all very interesting, but how does that prove the clue is in there?" Daniel asked, impatient for her to get to the point. He needed to get her out of the museum before the killer showed. That son of a bitch had slit the throats of too many innocent people already.

"There was a line in that pamphlet that reads, 'the story of the baptism at the River Jordan contains the key to True Faith.' I think he was hinting at the location."

"Why would he leave a clue to where he hid something?" the blonde Officer Smith asked.

Professor Laurent chuckled. "If you had studied the life of de Lacy, you wouldn't ask that. He was one of Europe's most famous eccentrics."

"Sorry we didn't study European eccentrics in the police academy," the other Officer Smith said.

The professor appeared too excited to notice the sarcasm.

Or maybe French snobbery doesn't realize it's being snobbish, Daniel mused.

"I can't believe I'm just inches away from one of the keys to the cryptex," she whispered.

Daniel cocked his head. That gleam in her eye … so obsessive. The killer probably had that same gleam, but with no heart or soul behind it. This cryptex legend really sunk its claws into people.

Edgar squinted through the glass at the icon. "But where's it hidden? Is there some writing in those reeds I'm not seeing?"

"Not a bad idea, but de Lacy was more subtle than that," Professor Laurent said. "See how thick the wood panel is? There must be a hidden space in there, something that flips open."

"And it hasn't been found in all this time?" The security guard sounded dubious.

"The niche was probably carved into it only a hundred years ago, and cleverly hidden before it went on display in the Cluny. The icon has probably only been handled two or three times since then," the professor said.

They all fell silent, peering at the front and sides.

"Too bad we can't see the bottom or the back," Daniel muttered. His curiosity had been piqued. After a moment, he began to look around at the room, figuring out where best to position himself and the two police officers. Except for an emergency exit in the back, the double doors into the exhibition were only one way in and out of this exhibition space. He'd post one officer in the stairwell of the emergency exit, and himself and the other officer behind two of the display cases on either side to flank the intruder.

The security guards he'd keep well out of the way in the camera room. He didn't want their blood on his conscience.

"Yes," Professor Laurent said quietly, as if to herself. "I'm sure this is the one."

"That's great, professor. We'll keep an eye on it. Why don't I take you to your car now?"

"Please let me have just a few minutes. I want to study it more closely and take some photos. I'll need to send a report to the Cluny, and they'll want details."

"This can wait until morning," one of the police officers said.

Professor Laurent ignored him, staring at Daniel with the eager, pleading eyes of a child desperate to stay up to watch her favorite TV show.

"All right," Daniel conceded after a moment. "Ten minutes. Then you're out of here."

He couldn't say no to Agent Nomellini's hellions either.

"Thank you," she whirled around and pressed her nose against the glass case, making her look even more like the eager child and less the esteemed academic.

Daniel chuckled and left her to it, wandering around the exhibition while idly looking at the great treasures of medieval France.

There had been a time when he had been almost as eager as her, or at least wanted someone to think he was.

All those European tours Mom had taken him on, and his undergraduate degree, weren't enough for him to cough up solutions to this riddle. He was glad he had found an expert.

Those European tours, they should have been the trips of a lifetime.

He found himself drawn to a large tripartite stained-glass window filling the wall near him, backlit to make it look like daylight was streaming through.

The center window showed an angel holding a censer, purifying the scene as he was flanked by some French king gripping a sword and his queen holding a model of a church, probably the one they built and in which this window had originally been. The angel was on a blue background, the monarchs on red backgrounds that seemed to compliment the central figure. Other bright colors enlivened the scene—the green of the angel's wings, the gold of the censor and crowns, the pure white of the angel's robe.

He remembered another stained-glass window, in another country, long ago …

"Sure is cool, Uncle Ray," twelve-year-old Daniel said.

He sat with his mom's boyfriend, who Daniel now happily called Uncle Ray after lots of fun trips to castles and ice cream parlors, in a medieval church in a little French village. They sat in one of the front pews, staring at a giant stained-glass window that had miraculously survived centuries of war and upheaval. The summer sun shone bright through the window, flooding the little church with color.

"Amazing, isn't it?" Uncle Ray said, putting an arm around him. "Look at that knight fighting the dragon in the center. Do you know who that is?"

"Saint George!"

"That's right, smart guy." Uncle Ray gave him a hug. Daniel basked in the attention. Dad had died when he was really, really young, so young he only had a few dim memories of him. He bet Dad had been a lot like Uncle Ray. Cool, and always ready to give him attention.

Not like Mom. Mom was always busy.

"Something strange about Saint George being here, isn't there?" Uncle Ray said.

Daniel's mind raced. He'd been taught this a couple of days ago. What was it? Right!

"Saint George is the patron saint of England!"

"You got it, little buddy. But we're in France. The truth is this church was built by the English when they controlled this part of France during the Hundred Years War. That stained glass window is a dead giveaway."

"Cool." Daniel looked around. "Gee, I'm surprised no one else is here."

Uncle Ray looked around too and hugged him closer.

"Yeah, little buddy," he said quietly. "Looks like we have this place all to ourselves."

"Impressive, isn't it?"

Daniel jolted out of the past, his hand going to the pistol in his shoulder holster.

Professor Laurent took half a step back. "Sorry if I startled you!"

"Oh, my bad," Daniel mumbled, looking down. "Stakeouts always get me jittery."

"Don't worry about it. I'm all done." She looked at the glowing window, a relic from centuries ago. "Beautiful, isn't it? Fifteenth century, during the great flowering of the art in France. I love how the artisan balanced the colors. It must have seemed glorious when the first light of dawn shone through it and into the church."

"I fucking hate stained glass," Daniel grumbled, and walked away, leaving Remi to stare after him openmouthed.

* * *

Remi sat in her car half a block down from the museum, far enough away that the security cameras wouldn't pick up that it was her car, and close enough that she could keep an eye on the place.

She was not going to just sit at home while law enforcement took away the one person who might know more about the cryptex than she did. Not before she got a chance to talk with him.

Just how she would handle the situation once it came up wasn't really clear in her mind. She had a vague idea of rushing in once she spotted the man trying to break into the museum. If she timed it right, she'd get there just as they grabbed him and just before they hauled him to the police station. That would be her chance. She just had to make it there at the right moment. Too late, and they'd be taking him away. Too early, and …

Remi shuddered. She didn't want to think about what might happen if she arrived on the scene too early.

So she waited down the street, her eyes on the museum.

She'd been waiting a couple of hours. She'd wait all night if she had to.

Unfortunately, her vantage point put her right next to the bar. People kept coming and going, mostly drunk men. She got several curious glances and more than one long leer.

Remi kept her phone to her ear as if she was talking. She felt tempted to actually call Agent Walker and keep him on the line, but he was busy on the stakeout and would wonder why she was calling. She couldn't exactly tell him that she had defied his orders to go home and was instead endangering herself.

There was something strange about that man. Strange and sad. When Remi had spotted him staring at that stained glass, he looked almost in tears, as if the beauty of it moved him. But then when she spoke a look of terror came to his face.

And then what he said afterwards made no sense. Who hates stained glass?

Who sits alone outside a cheap bar in a bad part of town hoping a serial killer shows up?

Her life had taken a very strange turn indeed.

Remi had never been terribly adventurous outside of the subjects she chose for her academic pursuits. But within those subjects, she was the most daring researcher she knew.

Ever since she was a little girl, Remi had always been fascinated with puzzles. Sudoku, crosswords, riddles, mathematical problems—it didn't matter as long as it was complicated. As long as it revealed an answer most people couldn't see.

So when she first heard of the cryptex as an undergraduate, from a mystical boyfriend who styled himself as a modern-day alchemist and took far too many magic mushrooms, she knew she wanted to write her thesis on the subject. The boyfriend was long gone, now living in an ashram in India, but her obsession with the cryptex remained.

It wasn't something she could speak of with ease. Her graduate committee rebuked her for taking on a subject they called "flighty" and almost didn't let her pass. Her colleagues praised her "more serious work" and fell into awkward silence when she brought up her passion. Even Cyril got uncomfortable and tried to change the subject.

But tonight, she had the chance to silence all the laughter, prove to the world that she wasn't some crackpot.

She could even solve a major crime at the same time.

A laughing crowd of middle-aged men came tumbling out of the bar, passing in front of her car. One turned, fixed his bleary gaze on her, and focused.

"Hey!" he shouted in exaggerated friendliness.

Remi tensed, pretending to be on the phone.

"You're still on the phone?" he asked, standing a few feet in front of her parked car. He turned to his friends. "She's still on the phone. She was on the phone when we went in."

Remi put her other hand in her purse to feel the reassuring shape of the small can of pepper spray.

"She's calling the cops on you!" one of the man's friends said. The crowd laughed.

"She's calling your momma to tell her what a drunk her son turned into!" the man shot back without heat. The crowd laughed again and stumbled away. Remi breathed a sigh of relief.

Then tensed all over again.

A dark figure was emerging from the side door of the museum.

She couldn't see clearly, but it was definitely a male, wearing a hooded sweatshirt.

Coming *out* of the museum. The killer had already been inside!

Desperately Remi called Agent Walker. The figure moved away from the museum …

… and toward Remi's parked car.

The FBI agent's phone rang once, twice. Why didn't he pick up on the first ring? Had he been hurt?

The figure continued to approach, walking quickly and carrying something.

Four rings. Five. Where the hell was Agent Walker?

"What is it?"

Remi almost sobbed with relief to hear his voice.

"Someone came out of the museum's east exit. A man in a hooded sweatshirt, coming down the street toward the bar."

"Damn it! What are you still doing here?"

"Never mind. Get out here and help!"

Remi could already hear him running. There was a crackle of a radio, words she couldn't catch. "Security says they haven't seen anyone pass by that camera."

"Well, I have. Get out here!"

"We're coming."

Not fast enough. The hooded figure passed by Remi's car on the opposite side of the street, heading away from the museum with long strides. He had a package about the size of a shoebox tucked under one arm. Just beyond where she was parked was a four-way intersection. If he took one of the turns, he'd be out of sight before the authorities even got out of the museum.

Remi stared. He was going to get away.

That package, it must be one of the clues to the cryptex. If he gets away, I'll never find it!

What to do? He didn't look like he had seen her. She was safe as long as she stayed in the car.

But he would be out of sight in less than a minute. They'd lose him.

Remi pulled the pepper spray out of her purse and reached for the door.

And paused.

What was she thinking? This man had already killed at least two people. And there was no one on the street. Did she think she could face down a serial killer with a little can of pepper spray?

He turned a corner, moving out of sight.

That decided it. She leapt out of the car and followed. She'd follow him, report on his position and keep him from getting away.

With her phone in one hand, primed to Agent Walker's number, and her pepper spray in the other, Remi ran to the corner, keeping close to the building so she would have cover. Once there, she peeked down the street.

The figure was already half a block away, having broken into a jog. Now he was angling across the street, heading for an alley.

No time to wait. No time even to call Agent Walker. She needed to act.

She hurried out into the street. The killer must have heard because he glanced nervously over his shoulder, spotting her.

A chill ran down her spine, making her hesitate again. For a moment they stared at each other from about thirty yards apart.

"I'm Professor Remi Laurent!" she called to him. She needed to talk to this man, no matter what the risk.

The figure hesitated, as if uncertain, then rushed into the alley.

"Hey!"

On impulse, Remi ran after him.

The alley was a wide one, leading through a block of shops to a street beyond. A few dumpsters stood there, and Remi's nostrils filled with the smell of trash and stale urine. She saw the figure running ahead of her. Her breath caught when she noticed he no longer carried the package.

Did he hide it?

She had begun to catch up, but it looked like he'd still make it out the other end of the alley well before her.

Until he turned around and stopped.

Remi stopped too, clutching her pepper spray. She felt a desperate urge to call Agent Walker but didn't dare take her eyes off the killer for an instant.

Then he ran for her, arms outstretched.

Remi screamed. She wanted to run but felt her legs frozen like twin pillars of ice. The figure rushed closer.

Just as he reached her, instinct kicked in and Remi sprayed a cloud of blinding, burning solution right into his face.

The man squalled, lashing out and clouting Remi on the side of the head.

The blow was more surprising than painful. Still, it made Remi stagger to the side.

The man groaned and wiped at his eyes, inadvertently knocking his hood off his head.

Remi blinked. It was the pimply young security guard.

This was the killer? It didn't make much sense.

"You bitch!" the guard shouted, trying to clear his eyes as he approached her.

Remi steadied herself and sprayed him again.

He stumbled past her, nearly bowling her over, and tried to run away. In his confusion he ended up heading back in the direction from which they came.

This guy isn't the murderer. Is he an accomplice?

Emboldened that he didn't have any weapon, Remi grabbed onto the back of his hoodie with both hands and tried to drag him down. The man staggered but did not fall. Instead, he thrashed about wildly, catching Remi in the temple with an elbow.

The historian saw stars. The next thing she knew, she was on her knees and the security guard, rubbing his half-blinded eyes and still squalling like a baby, hurried toward the end of the alley.

Another figure appeared at the end of the alley, backlit by the streetlight. In the silhouette she could clearly see the gun in his hand.

Remi's heart clenched. Did the security guard have backup? Was this the actual killer?

The guard saw the newcomer too late. He stopped for a second, then tried to barrel through.

The newcomer swung the butt of his pistol down on the security guard's skull, dropping him to the filthy pavement.

The man with the pistol leaned over the security guard, and as he did the streetlight illuminated his face.

It was Agent Walker. Remi burst into a smile.

"You're under arrest," the FBI agent said, flipping the half-conscious security guard onto his front and cuffing him.

Leaning against the brick wall, Remi got to her feet.

"We got him," she gasped.

The sound of running feet made them both turn. One of the Officers Smith, Remi couldn't tell which in the half light and didn't care, appeared at the end of the alley.

"Take care of him," Agent Walker said, gesturing at the prone form of the security guard. "I'll take care of the professor."

“I’m fine,” Remi said, but nevertheless took the FBI’s arm when he offered it.

“Fine? You’re crazy is what you are. You could have been killed.”

Remi shuddered. As the agent’s words sank in, she shuddered again.

And found she couldn’t stop.

CHAPTER NINE

The Virginia Museum of Fine Arts in Richmond had closed its doors hours before. Now the halls were dim, the displays unlit, and the museum entirely quiet except for the soft cursing of Mortimer Phelps.

Mortimer hated his job as a security guard. Long hours, boring work, low pay, and the disdain of everybody around you. Not like being a police officer.

He had always dreamed of being a police officer. When Mortimer was a kid and he and his pals played cops and robbers, he always volunteered to be the cop, and complained when it was the robbers' turn to win. He'd studied Criminal Justice in college and graduated with honors. Right after the graduation ceremony, he had shucked off his robe and mortarboard and made a beeline for the nearest police academy.

Only to get rejected because he had asthma and a herniated disc.

He'd known about both ailments, of course, and had tried to hide them in the physical. The doctor had caught him out and told Mortimer in no uncertain terms that he would never be a police officer.

At 21, with his whole life ahead of him, he had been barred from his dream.

And now, twenty years later, he was stuck in an art museum at two in the morning scrubbing off graffiti tags in the Fabergé Egg Room.

And why was a security guard stuck wiping off graffiti instead of doing his rounds? Because the damn janitors were on strike.

Mortimer Phelps cursed louder and scrubbed harder. This was last of four tags some punk kid had sprayed on the walls and display cases of the room before one of his daytime colleagues tackled him.

"Plut," it said in big puffy white letters. Was that even a word?

It sure meant something to the eighteen-year-old loser who wrote it. Mortimer had seen Plut tags all over town.

Now the punk was spending the night in jail. Mortimer hoped some snaggle-toothed axe murderer forced the brat to be his girlfriend.

As Mortimer scrubbed harder, he wished for the hundredth time that he had been on daytime duty. He would have tackled the kid before he'd even gotten his spray can out of the bag and would have given him a couple of gut punches once he was down. Teach the brat a lesson.

Mortimer stopped to wipe his brow. He needed to take a breather and step away from the cleaning supplies. Sometimes it set off his asthma. The mask he wore should help but he worried that wearing it for too long a stretch might also set off his asthma.

He could have used his condition as a way to get out of cleaning duty, but he had never told his employers about it. Too embarrassing.

Mortimer tore off his mask, wiped the sweat from around his mouth, and took a casual glance around the room showcasing five Fabergé eggs. The largest collection outside of Russia, the museum liked to brag.

Mortimer didn't know why everyone thought they were so special. Sure, they were worth a lot of money and he supposed they took some skill to make. He got it. But they were too ornate, too arsty-fartsy. One was all gold with so many designs on it you had to stare at it a good five minutes to see it all. And for some reason it had an enamel pelican on the top feeding her young in a little nest.

Why would a pelican sit on top of an egg that was ten times its size? It didn't make any sense.

At least it wasn't as bad as the so-called Peter the Great Egg, which someone had told him hadn't even been made for Peter the Great, whoever the hell that was. This one was even more complicated, with all sorts of swirly designs and rubies and diamonds and stuff around a little painting of a palace. The painting was so small you could barely see any details of the palace.

What was the point? Whoever made this should have spent the money on a proper-sized painting so you could actually see what the palace looked like and save the gems to make rings for all the cute babes who hung around the palace. Stupid Russkies.

And then there was that egg over there …

A crash echoed through the empty halls and rooms, making Mortimer spin around, his hand going to the revolver at his belt.

For a second, Mortimer didn't move.

React, dumbass. It's him!

Mortimer always read the crime news, and so he knew two other museums had been broken into. He'd studied all the grisly details of the crimes, had warned his colleagues about it even before the museum administration had said anything.

Despite feeling certain that the Security Guard Slasher, as Mortimer had dubbed him, was even now stalking the halls of The Virginia Museum of Fine Arts, Mortimer did not feel much fear.

Instead, he felt elated.

Now's my chance.

Drawing his gun, he ducked to the side of the doorway to keep out of sight.

He cocked his ear and listened. Nothing.

That had sounded like some sort of metal smashing. So not a display case. Of course, a good thief could get into a display case without much noise, and this guy was a good thief. He had disabled the security systems and picked the locks in two other museums, and he had obviously just done the same in this one.

A good thief wouldn't have made so much noise after taking so much care to sneak in.

That confirmed Mortimer's theory of the Security Guard Slasher.

He didn't just want to break artifacts, he wanted to kill security guards.

That crash of metal was supposed to bring Mortimer running. Then the killer would leap out from some hiding place, grab him from behind, and slit his throat.

Mortimer's free hand strayed to the walkie talkie at his belt. Should he call Finch? The other night watchman would be doing his rounds and should be somewhere on the ground floor right about now. The guy probably hadn't even heard the noise.

No, he wouldn't call Finch. The guy was getting a bit long in the tooth and would be no good in a fight. Calling poor old Finch would only endanger his life.

Call the cops? No. They'd never make it in time. It was up to Mortimer Phelps, the man everyone passed over for the police academy. The man everyone thought of as nothing but a museum security guard.

Standing a little straighter, he checked his revolver. Mortimer had been through several humiliating security jobs before finding one that let him carry a gun. While he had never used it, he always kept it clean and spent hours every week practicing at the range.

Puffing out his chest, Mortimer gathered his courage and snuck out of the Fabergé Egg Room.

The sound had come from the east wing, where the medieval collection was. The killer seemed to have a thing for the knights and castles stuff. He'd be lying somewhere in wait, ready to pounce on Mortimer when he came running.

So he wouldn't come running. Mortimer went in the opposite direction, passing through a staff door that took him to a series of labs and storage rooms extending the length of the building's interior. He could pass through these all the way to the other side of the museum and come at the medieval section from the other side.

The killer wouldn't be expecting that. He must have scoped Mortimer's position before making that noise. Easy enough. The Fabergé Egg Room was the only one that was fully lit.

The idea that the killer had been watching him as he scrubbed the damn tags off the walls gave Mortimer the chills.

Get a hold of yourself.

The windowless labs and storage rooms were pitch black, and Mortimer didn't dare switch on the lights in case the killer spotted the light under one of the staff doors, so Mortimer put his flashlight on its lowest setting and made his way through the rooms by its dim glow. Dark forms of statues loomed over him, and stacks of boxes gave a killer a thousand places to hide. Mortimer kept a tight grip on his gun.

Once he got in position at a staff door two rooms away from the medieval section, he pressed his ear against it for a moment. No sound. The guy was still waiting. He must be wondering if Mortimer had heard him.

Setting the flashlight on a shelf next to the door—he didn't dare holster his pistol—he reached for the doorknob, his sweat-slick hand slipping on the brass.

Mortimer wiped his hand on his brown polyester pants and turned the knob, peeking out.

The Early Religious Art section was quiet. A small light in each room remained on all night, giving him just enough light to see. He switched his flashlight off so as not to signal his approach.

From his vantage point, he could not see the open doorway leading to the second room of this section, and the open doorway beyond that leading to the first of three medieval rooms.

Easing the door open, he slipped through, then tiptoed to the side of the doorway. Listening again, he thought he heard something, the soft rustle of clothing as someone adjusted position.

He might be in the next room, waiting for me.

Time to be a hero.

Mortimer swung around the side of the doorway, pistol leveled.

Nothing.

This room had several display cases standing in two rows. Plenty of hiding places. Mortimer kept to the left-hand wall to flank the killer's position in case he was hiding behind one of them. While Mortimer had outflanked the guy, all it would take would be one wrong move and the Security Guard Killer would be on to him. His eyes darted from shadow to shadow, knowing that at any moment the maniac might leap out of one of them.

Step by step, he crept forward, ears straining for the slightest sound.

Good thing Finch isn't here. With those arthritic knees he'd be clacking with every step and telling the whole museum where he was.

Finch! I forgot to turn off my walkie talkie! If he calls. I'm a dead man.

Mortimer looked down at his walkie talkie and saw the little green light that indicated it was on.

The little green light shining in the dark room.

Mortimer grimaced and turned off the walkie talkie with an audible click.

He almost didn't hear the movement behind him as the dark figure of a man leaped from his hiding place behind one of the display cases and rushed him.

Mortimer spun and pulled the trigger just as the man slammed into him. The gun barked, and a moment later he felt a hot pain as a knife cut into his side.

Then he fell, back slamming against the tile floor, sending a sharp pain down his spine as his herniated disc took the impact.

For a second, he could do nothing except blearily watch the man in the overalls and boots clap a hand to his shoulder and come away with blood.

He looked straight at Mortimer, and the fury in those eyes made him catch his breath …

… and not get it back.

He wheezed, gulping for air as his asthma kicked in.

Not now!

With no time to grab his inhaler, he leveled his gun. His aim wobbled as his chest heaved. Stars appeared in his eyes, his peripheral vision tunneling.

The killer roared and came at him.

Mortimer fired twice, missing both times.

The knife came down.

Mortimer rolled away, noticing the broken reliquary on the floor nearby.

He screamed as the knife stabbed through his calf. Mortimer dropped his gun and it bounced on the tile out of reach.

The killer yanked out the knife. Mortimer struggled to get to his revolver, just inches out of his grasp. A rush of sound made him roll away, the knife screeching against the tile inches from his neck.

He rolled right into the reliquary.

Still gasping for breath, he grabbed it, struggling to his knees and ignoring the sharp pain in his back. The killer stalked toward him. Mortimer tried to focus as his vision dimmed and agony encompassed his entire being.

Again, the knife came down. Mortimer lifted the reliquary as a shield and blocked the blow. With what remained of his sight, he noticed that the killer had actually stabbed into the open box, putting his whole hand inside.

A clever move Mortimer had seen in a martial arts movie came to him. He twisted the box, twisting the killer's wrist as he did so, then swung the gold box against the side of the killer's head.

Box and skull connected with a satisfying smack, and the killer staggered to the side.

Don't underestimate Mortimer Phelps!

A clatter of metal in front of him made him look down.

The knife! The loser dropped his knife!

Wheezing hard now, Mortimer grabbed it with the last of his strength.

Just as he did so, the killer kicked him hard in the side, making him drop it again.

The killer reached down to pick it up and Mortimer belted him one right in the wounded shoulder.

That got an anguished cry, followed quickly by a howl of rage.

The knife slashed across Mortimer's chest. The security guard twisted and fell onto his front. Through fading vision, he saw his gun and scrambled in that direction.

He never made it. The cruel blade came down again, this time square in his back.

Mortimer groaned. The pain began to ebb, and the light grew dim as the knife plunged into his back again and again.

At least I hurt him, Mortimer thought. *I felt blood when I punched that gunshot wound on his shoulder. Maybe he'll bleed out. Even if he doesn't, at least he'll never be able to forget Mortimer Phelps.*

At least I died a hero.

Mortimer Phelps died with a smile on his face.

CHAPTER TEN

An hour later, in the waiting room of the local precinct, Daniel crossed his arms, anger simmering inside him, and glared at Professor Laurent.

"What the hell did you think you were doing?" he demanded.

The professor looked equal parts abashed, shocked, and defiant. She twiddled a cup of the horrible coffee that it was traditional to give everyone who entered a police station. She had a bruise on her temple from where the security guard hit her.

"I couldn't sit by while you arrested him," she said, looking at the floor. "I needed to talk with him first."

"This is a serial killer; you don't just sit down and have a friendly little chat about history!"

The professor's eyes sparked. "This is more than a 'little chat;' it's one of the biggest mysteries of European civilization."

"You could have been killed."

"But I wasn't. He would have gotten away if it wasn't for me."

Daniel suppressed a smile. The professor had actually kicked ass. The perp got such a hefty dose of pepper spray that he could barely see. He even ran off in the wrong direction!

This woman was more than just a snooty academic, although she was certainly that too.

"You did good," Daniel conceded, keeping his voice hard. "But you shouldn't have been there. He could have cut you to pieces."

Professor Laurent trembled a little. "You came just at the right time. Thank you."

Daniel nodded. "You're an interesting person, professor. The world is better off with you around."

That brought a smile from her. Daniel almost smiled back, then said,

"This isn't a game. From now on you have to listen to me. Understood?"

"I understand. Sorry. I forgot myself." Then the professor's brow furrowed. "He didn't seem to have a knife."

"We didn't recover one at the scene." That struck Daniel as odd. Actually, several things about the suspect did. His build was wrong, and he didn't strike him as the killer type. Hopefully they could clear that up. The perp was being processed right now. Once done, they'd stick him in an interrogation room and pump him.

"How come you didn't see him on the camera?" the professor asked. "Did Edgar and the other guard fall asleep or something?"

Daniel shrugged. "He insists no one came through the door."

"That's strange."

"Maybe not. Since he had access to the cameras, he could have put them on a prerecorded loop to show no activity."

"Oh. Why didn't you see him when he came into the exhibition?"

"Because he didn't." That was another strange thing about this.

And there were more odd aspects about the perp. George Hansen was a second-year college student majoring in computer programming. From the little Daniel had time to get from Edgar and the other security guard, George was sociable, lived with his parents, and showed no strong religious convictions.

That was the exact opposite of the profile Daniel was beginning to create about the Cryptex Killer. The man was an obsessive, so probably a loner. Given the nature of the cryptex, he was most likely deeply religious, although perhaps not in any standard religion but in the occult. He was also older. It took time to develop the skills that he had shown, probably as a licensed contractor. And while the images they had of him on the CCTV from the other two museums were poor at best, they showed the deliberate movements of a mature man.

George did not fit. Was he a sidekick to the real killer? While serial killers usually worked alone, such a thing was not unheard of.

The blonde Officer Smith poked his head in the room.

"The suspect is in Interrogation Room One. Since this is the FBI's case, I guess you want to take the lead in this."

"Thanks. The backup units in place in the museum?"

"Yep. We got four officers there now, two standing by that display at all times."

"Great. I'll be right along."

The police officer left. Daniel turned to the professor.

"Got to go. Why don't you go home? We can take your statement in the morning."

"Wait! I still want to question him."

Daniel made an emphatic shake of his head. "No way."

"He's not dangerous now, and I might be able to dig up things you can't. He must know me."

"It's not procedure."

A sly smile came to Professor Laurent's lips. "Since when did you care about that?"

Daniel chuckled. "You might have a bright future as an FBI profiler. OK, you can sit and watch from the observation room. If you want to say something, send me a text, but only if you have something vital to ask. Interrogations are delicate procedures and if you interrupt at the wrong time or say the wrong thing, it can derail the whole process."

"All right. I'll try not to interrupt."

"Pretend you're a student in one of your own lectures."

"You mean I should sit there texting and not paying attention?"

Daniel laughed. "OK, bad analogy. Let's go."

They passed down the hall, the blonde Officer Smith rejoining them.

"Since you made the collar, how about you play bad cop and I'll play good cop?" the policeman suggested.

"Makes sense," Daniel agreed.

"Policemen actually do that?" Professor Laurent asked.

"We eat donuts too," Daniel said.

"Really?"

"Actually no, I prefer Twinkies," Daniel said.

"I'm a Ho-Hos man myself," Officer Smith said.

Daniel gave him a high five.

He showed her into the observation room, a darkened room looking through one way glass into the interrogation room, then he and the cop went next door.

The interrogation room, a blank concrete rectangle with a desk and a few chairs bolted to the floor so they couldn't be used as weapons. George Hansen sat handcuffed to one, shoulders slumped, an untouched cup of undrinkable police coffee in front of him. He looked small, young, and vulnerable. One leg jerked up and down.

Looking at this poor sap, Daniel felt even more doubt than before.

But he couldn't show that. He had to play bad cop.

"Here he is, ladies and gentlemen," Daniel announced as he came in the room. "The Cryptex Killer!"

George's head shot up, eyes going wide. "Killer? I didn't kill anyone!"

Daniel leaned in close, glaring at him. "But your buddy did, didn't he? He hired you to take the cryptex clue from this museum, because you were the inside man. Made it safer for him. Must have hurt his pride not being able to slit a security guard's throat. He's killed two already and since you're helping him, that makes you an accessory to two counts of murder."

"Murder? Accessory?" George looked utterly confused.

"As well as theft, breaking and entering, assault, and resisting arrest."

George glanced at the cop, who stood nearby wearing a sympathetic look. "I didn't mean to hit her. She grabbed me and maced me! And I sure never killed anybody!"

No you didn't, did you?

You lost a fight with a female academic, after all.

"Your pal did," Daniel went on. "Why don't you tell us about him?"

"Pal? What pal?"

Officer Smith sat on the desk near the prisoner. "Look, we know you're not a killer. You had plenty of chance to kill your coworkers, but you didn't. And maybe you're scared—"

"Scared? Hell yeah I'm scared. You guys are saying—"

Officer Smith rolled over him. "Scared of the real killer. Who wouldn't be? The guy's obviously a psycho, and with his skills he can get at you anywhere. Maybe he pressured you into this, threatened you and your family."

Realization dawned. "Wait. Are you talking about that dude who killed those security guards in those other museums? The dude you were staking out? You think I have something to do with that?"

"We know you do," Daniel growled. "We have a heap of evidence on you."

George tried to raise his hands to object got caught short by the length of chain connecting his handcuffs to the chair. The rattle sounded loud in the cramped room.

"I stole some stuff to pay for college! I'm sorry! I didn't want to be stuck with debt when I graduate. I got $20,000 in student loans already."

"So you robbed the museum when the police and FBI were staking the place out?" Daniel barked. "How stupid do you think we are?"

Not as stupid as I think you are.

And the killer isn't stupid. God, I wish he was.

"You guys were distracted guarding the temporary exhibition, so I figured no one would notice me going into storage and taking some Roman bronzes. We got dozens of them that just sit in storage. No one sees them. They never go on display. Museums got more stuff in storage then they do behind glass. I figured no one would miss them, and I could sell them to someone who appreciates them. A victimless crime."

"So how did you do it?" Officer Smith asked.

"Earlier tonight I looped some old recordings of the east staff entrance so it would look like no one passed through. When it was my turn to go on rounds, I grabbed the bronzes and went out. I told everyone my car was in the shop and I had to take the bus to work, but really I had parked it a couple of blocks away. I was going to put the Roman stuff in the trunk and come back before anyone missed me."

"The professor here says you had a box under your arm," Daniel said.

George nodded eagerly. "That was it."

"She also said it disappeared in the moment when she lost sight of you."

"I stashed it in the alley."

Daniel nodded. That's what they had figured. They had sent the other Officer Smith to go look for it. He was taking his sweet time getting back, though.

George continued to babble about how he had nothing to do with the other two break-ins. Daniel sat back, letting Officer Smith do the questioning. The more he looked at this kid, the less he thought he was the killer or even in with the killer. It just didn't fit.

Officer Smith stopped his questioning as his phone buzzed. He looked at it, glanced at Daniel, and nodded toward the door. They headed out, closing the door on a despondent George Hansen.

Professor Laurent popped out of the observation room and joined them.

"My colleague retrieved the stolen items," the cop told them as they went down the hall.

The brown-haired Officer Smith stood at the front desk with a small cardboard box.

"That looks like the box the security guard was carrying," Professor Laurent said.

"I found it stashed in the alley where you bagged him," the police officer said.

"What took you so long?" Daniel asked. "We sent you to look for it an hour ago."

The cop shrugged. "And I went. But when I got there, I had to break up a fight. I brought the two guys in, processed them, and went back out. Just in time to stop some drunk from that bar by the museum from assaulting a woman. So I had to arrest him and processes him, and take the woman's statement."

Daniel glanced at the professor, who had turned pale. Officer Smith went on.

"Then I finally got to go back for your stupid box. Here it is."

"That's too small to be the icon," the professor said.

"We were watching the icon the whole time," Daniel said.

"He must have taken the clue out beforehand and was waiting for the right time to sneak off with it," she suggested.

Daniel moved over and opened the box. The professor peered over his shoulder. Inside were five bronze Roman statuettes.

Everyone let out a breath of disappointment.

"Looks like the kid was telling the truth," the blonde Officer Smith said.

"These look pretty solid," Daniel said. He picked one up, hefted its weight, and turned it over, looking for any marks that might act as a clue. "I don't think anything could be hidden in them. But could they hold some clue just from their shape, like that other Roman object?"

Professor Laurent shook her head. "No. All the stories associated with the cryptex say it was made by Christians. Yes, they dabbled in the occult, but their theology was based on Medieval Christianity. They would not have used pagan figurines." Suddenly she got a worried look. "Maybe the killer was using George Hansen as a decoy. He could be breaking in there right now!"

The other Officer Smith raised a hand. "Don't worry. We got four other officers there now."

"We should go back," Professor Laurent said. "The real killer might come in at any moment."

"I'll go back," Daniel said. "You'll go home. And no sneaking around the museum this time. Sounds like the night's really kicked off down there."

"We'll both go," the professor demanded, jutting out her chin.

Daniel tried not to smile.

This woman's got some spirit. Still, she's been knocked around once tonight already.

"You can't come. That's final."

"I'll stay outside. I have my pepper spray."

"Didn't you unload it on that stupid kid in there?"

"I still have some left."

The blonde Officer Smith came to Daniel's rescue.

"We still haven't taken your statement, Ms. Laurent. How about we sit down and do that while the events are fresh in your memory?"

The cop and Daniel exchanged a glance, and Daniel knew that the statement would take as long as Officer Smith could stretch it out.

Professor Laurent wasn't fooled. She rounded on the police officer. "Absolutely not. You're not keeping me here when there's more important work to be done."

Officer Smith kept his patience. "Ma'am, refusing to give a statement can be construed as—"

Daniel's phone rang. Gratefully he picked it up to be out of the professor's line of fire.

He saw it was the central office. Damn, this late at night? It couldn't be good news.

He picked up.

"Agent Daniel Walker of the Antiquities Division?"

Daniel crinkled his nose. He still didn't like the sound of that. He was from the Behavioral Affairs Unit, damn it!

"Yes," he grumbled.

"This is the central office. We've just been informed there was another break-in and murder at a museum. It just occurred at The Virginia Museum of Fine Arts in Richmond. We don't have details from the local PD as of yet, but it appears to be the same suspect you're hunting."

Daniel felt a cold feeling in the pit of his gut. His head felt light, as if detached from his body and the rest of the room. He leaned on the wall for support.

"We got it wrong," he whispered. "We got it all wrong."

Professor Laurent stepped closer to him, her face drawn. "What happened?"

"He hit a museum in Richmond. Killed a guard."

The professor let out a little cry and brought her hands to her face. "It's my fault."

Daniel shook his head, a sick feeling in his gut. "No, it's my fault. I should have seen more clearly. But how can I? This guy moves so damn fast. I've never come across a serial killer who moves this fast."

Frustration welled up in him. Generally, it took months to build a profile and nab a killer. Sometimes years. Because most serial killers only killed every few weeks or months.

This guy was killing practically every other day.

Impossible. It's impossible for me to get him before he strikes again.

Daniel launched himself off the wall and headed out of the room.

"I got to go."

"Wait! I'm coming with you," Professor Laurent said, catching up with him.

Daniel glanced at her and saw in her face the same look of guilt and shock that must have been on his own.

"I want to help," the professor said. "I *can* help. I made a mistake. Let me correct it."

If you say no, she'll have to live with the guilt. And maybe she'll come up with some useful ideas. Sure, she messed up this time, but that's not her fault. She has no training and is running under the clock.

And you messed up too.

"It's going to be hard," he told her.

The professor's head bowed. "It already is hard."

"It's going to get harder."

She looked up at him, and the hardness in her eyes almost made him jump.

"I don't care. I need to see this through to the finish."

Daniel studied her for a moment.

She has what it takes. I think.

Only one way to find out.

"Let's go," was all he said.

Then they hurried out the door.

CHAPTER ELEVEN

The next morning, the police didn't allow Remi into the room at The Virginia Museum of Fine Arts until they had taken away the body. For that she felt grateful. The chalk outline of where it had lain and the blood spattered all over the floor was enough.

There was so much of it. Remi didn't need to be an FBI agent to see what had happened. Through bleary eyes, untouched by sleep, Remi saw two spatters of blood in one room—one small and one large. From the large one ran a regular trail into the next room, then a large pool around where the chalk outline was on the floor.

This was done by the person I thought I was chasing last night. I could have ended up like this.

Remi shuddered.

A little beyond the pool of dried blood stood an open display cabinet. At its base lay 15th century English reliquary, its delicate gold top smashed open to reveal a secret compartment large enough to hold something the size of a deck of cards. The bone of the saint the reliquary contained lay pulverized on the floor.

That desecration of human remains, and of a priceless object of art, usually would have sickened her. But she could not keep her eyes off the pool of blood and the outline of where a man had been butchered.

He died because I couldn't see clearly. He died because the killer is more intelligent than I am.

If I hadn't led them to the wrong museum, that poor man might be alive right now. Agent Walker might have come up with a different conclusion. He might have guessed the right museum.

What am I doing here? I have no idea how to hunt a murderer.

Remi kept a Kleenex up against her mouth, worried she might be sick. Agent Walker was conferring with the CSI team and a local homicide detective. She had trouble focusing on their conversation.

The CSI team spoke to each other in clipped, technical terms Remi didn't understand, hardly exchanging a complete sentence. They were a tight unit, not needing to explain things to one another as they went about their grisly work with quiet efficiency.

Not like the museum director, a red-nosed old Southern gentleman with swept back white hair and a summer suit of a cheery yellow that looked disrespectful considering their grim surroundings.

"It's all my fault!" he cried, waving his arms with exaggerated motions. "I heard about the other murders and didn't take precautions. I thought that with so many art museums in the country, what were the chances? Besides, our security guards are armed, not like at the Cloisters or Glencairn."

Agent Walker spoke to him in a quiet, level tone, obviously trying to calm him down. "Why do they carry revolvers?"

"My predecessor issued them guns after a horrible break-in fifteen years ago in which a guard and a docent were tied up and beaten. More than three million dollars' worth of art was stolen. The police never traced the art."

Remi noted that the museum director sounded more distraught over the missing art than the beaten employees.

"This gold box, how long has it been in your collection?" Agent Walker asked.

"The reliquary of St. Anselm of Canterbury? I'm not sure. I'll have to look it up."

It was donated to the museum in 1932 by a member of the Cryptex Club, you fool, Remi thought. *And you never noticed that hidden compartment in the lid that I can see from where I'm standing.*

Of course, the lid hadn't been smashed open before.

Agent Walker handed him a card.

"Please send me that information, as well as where it came from. Is that bone real?" The FBI agent pointed to the crushed bone next to the broken reliquary.

The museum director ran his fingers through his hair. "Yes, it is. It's believed to be the leg bone of St. Anselm himself. Who would do such a thing!"

Yes, who would do such a thing? Remi wondered. *He must have something against religion. But wait, that doesn't make sense considering what he's hunting.*

She stared at the broken reliquary, wondering what had been hidden inside, and felt a strange spike of jealousy. It should have been *her* making the discovery. *She* should have been the one to track down all the clues.

Agent Walker ignored the museum director's question and asked one of his own. "Did you know there was a secret compartment in the top of that reliquary?"

"No. I had no idea. It makes no sense. Reliquaries are to show off saints' bones, not hide them."

"I doubt it was a bone. An officer from the local PD is checking your security footage. I'll have him send me what he finds. Do you know anyone who has a grudge against the museum? Or against Mr. Phelps, the security guard?"

"No. I mean, there is no shortage of rivalry and petty backbiting in the art world. A lot of money is involved. Combine that with inflated egos and you get quite the toxic mix. But murder? Breaking a priceless artifact? Stomping on the bone of a saint? This is the work of a madman!"

A madman who is more clever than me or Agent Walker, Remi thought. *He's staying one step ahead of us.*

Or more.

"I'll be in touch," Agent Walker said.

At last, he came over to her.

"Looks like it's our man. Same M.O. Disabled the security cameras and the alarm system. The victim fought back, though. CSI showed me three bullet marks on the far wall of the other room, and one of the bloodstains is consistent with the killer getting shot. There wasn't much blood, looks like he just got grazed, but enough to get a DNA sample."

"What good is a DNA sample unless we catch him?" Remi asked, unable to take her eyes off the blood and the white outline in the middle of it.

"We can run the DNA through our database. If he's committed a major crime in the last few years, we'll get him. Serial killers generally escalate to their killing sprees, starting with juvenile delinquency and graduating to affray or assault. If we're lucky, we can find a match."

"And if we're unlucky?" Remi asked.

Daniel bent a little so her lowered gaze would meet his eyes. "Then I keep hunting for him."

"*We* keep hunting for him," she corrected.

Until she said it, she didn't know the words would come out of her mouth.

Was that a spark of admiration she saw in Agent Walker's eye?

He shouldn't be so generous.

"I-I need to see this through," she stammered. "I miscalculated somewhere. I thought he'd hit Washington, D.C. next, and never even thought about this museum. It's my fault that poor man is dead."

Remi choked back a sob.

The FBI agent put a hand on her shoulder. "Hey. Don't beat yourself up over it. We all make mistakes in this job. We're searching in the dark, trying to second guess complete strangers with mental problems. I've stumbled before, and that's cost lives. It's hard to live with, but I've learned to live with it."

Remi stared at him, moved that this rude American was suddenly acting so caring. "How?"

Agent Walker stood a little straighter. "By always getting the guy in the end. You keep at him and keep at him and until all the little bits of evidence fall into place and you figure it out."

"It sounds exhausting. I've been doing this for less than two days and I'm already worn out."

"It is exhausting. And frustrating. And sometimes it can get really dangerous. All my friends and family have told me to quit. But I keep at it because it's important. We're saving lives. Nothing more important than that."

Remi smiled a more genuine smile this time, catching the "we."

"So you think I can still be of use even though I made a big mistake?"

"Especially because of it. We need to figure out why he skipped Washington, D.C. First he hit New York. Then Pennsylvania. Then he skipped to Richmond. Why? D.C. is on the way. Why not hit that first, especially since the D.C. show is ending soon?"

Remi slumped. "I don't know."

Agent Walker took his hand off her shoulder. "You will. You know this stuff better than anyone. I need you. Can you get leave from your classes? I can call the university administration if you need me to. I've had to do it before. If a boss causes any trouble, a call from the FBI always straightens him out."

"If you could do that, it would help. It would be hard for me to explain."

If I told them I was hunting the cryptex for the federal government, they'd just laugh behind my back like always.

He isn't laughing, though.

"All right. I'll call them right after we get out of here. Then we'll get to work. Sounds good?"

Remi shook her head. "No, it sounds dreadful."

The FBI agent let out a bitter laugh. "Now you're getting the hang of it. You'll be just fine on this job."

Remi looked him in the eye. "Thank you, Daniel."

The nod he gave in response was curt, but she saw friendliness there. And respect.

"No problem, Remi. Let's go get some breakfast. You look like you need a coffee. Or two. I sure as hell do."

* * *

"Now I know why I guessed the wrong museum," Remi said.

Remi and Daniel sat in that American war crime against international cuisine—the diner. They'd sped down to The Virginia Museum of Fine Arts as soon as Daniel got the call in the early hours of this morning and hadn't eaten since.

So, once they had finished up at the museum, Daniel had taken her here for a late breakfast.

And ordered a bacon double cheeseburger.

For breakfast.

The sight of all that blood had put her off her appetite, and Daniel munching away on a greasy slab of processed meat wasn't exactly helping, so Remi busied herself draining her third coffee and working on her laptop.

"Look at this article," she said, turning her laptop to face the FBI agent.

"X-Ray Analysis of the de Lacy Icon of the Cluny Museum, Paris," Daniel read around a mouthful of carcinogens.

"Someone at the University of Florence x-rayed the icon searching for secret niches, just like I suspected there might be."

"And?"

"And nothing. She found nothing." Remi felt a tug of disappointment. She had felt so sure.

"So there was nothing there in the first place. I guess that's why the killer didn't go for it."

"There's more to it than that," Remi said, pulling away her laptop as Daniel took another bite and made a glop of ketchup shoot out the side of the burger and land perilously close to her computer. "I had written in one of my older articles that I believed the de Lacy collection contained one of the clues. I hadn't made the connection to the icon, which I should have considering what I knew about de Lacy."

"But this Italian researcher did?"

"Yes. So she analyzed the icon and found no hidden niches. But here's what's important about that. This article was only published a week ago. I've been so busy I hadn't even noticed it."

"But our knife wielding maniac friend obviously had," Daniel said.

That got an odd look from the next booth. Remi blushed and lowered her voice.

"Yes. He's keeping track of anything published that has to do with the cryptex. But this isn't an article you can simply find on a website. This was from JSTOR."

"I've heard of that. It's an academic database, right?"

"That's right. It's mostly for academic journals. More importantly, it's subscription only."

Light dawned in Daniel's face. "See, I told you that you were useful to have around."

Remi managed a little laugh despite the exhaustion and shock of the previous evening. Just thinking about it made her heart race. Drinking too much coffee probably didn't help matters. "JSTOR isn't just subscription only. Few people have private accounts since it's so expensive. Subscription tends to be through a university, which then allows its students and faculty to use it. But they have to use their ID to log in, and only when they're on campus. You can't access it remotely."

"Oh. Wow. Hold on. I got to send an email to Cybercrime." He put down his burger, did a poor job of wiping his hands, grabbed his phone, and started to type. "They can track this guy in no time. Give me some of the keywords he would have used. Cryptex, obviously, but what else?"

Remi thought for a second. "De Lacy. Code. Cryptography. Cluny. Medieval. Cryptex Club. Sofia Romano, that's the author of this paper. Harold Wagner, an important early researcher from a few decades ago. Um, let's see …"

Daniel looked up from his phone. "Remi Laurent."

Remi winced. "Yes. I suppose that's one of his most common searches."

Daniel typed it in. "This will be good for starters. It shouldn't be too hard. The only problem is we'll need to get a warrant from a judge to search JSTOR's database. That should be fast-tracked thanks to the nature of the case but add in delays from the database company and we might not have our answer until tomorrow or the day after tomorrow."

Remi felt herself going pale. "Giving him time to commit another murder."

"Then we need to get cracking. It's morning. We have until night. Maybe more. The next museum might be in California for all we know. Or England. Plus, he got shot. We don't know how badly. It might slow him down."

"My sister is a physician in Paris. She told me they have to report all gunshot and knife wounds to the police. Is it the same here?"

Daniel blinked. "Why wouldn't it be?"

Remi looked uncomfortable. "Well, you have so many more of them."

"Oh. Yeah." Europe's violent crime rate was way lower than the United States. "Well, we do require hospitals to report those kinds of wounds, and we're watching that. I doubt he'll go to the emergency room, though. Too risky."

"But he might have to."

"Probably not. The CSI guys say there wasn't too much blood. He probably got grazed. It might scare him a bit, though, make him more cautious."

Remi looked down at the table. "And even more dangerous."

And if he has been reading my work, he might have as much of an obsession about me as he does about the cryptex. What if we really do cross paths? What would that kind of man do then?

CHAPTER TWELVE

The Chosen One sat in the grimy bathroom of a cheap motel where the management accepted cash and did not require photo ID. Gingerly he peeled off the gauze he had put on his shoulder right after he had escaped the museum and examined the wound.

A shallow furrow ran along the flesh of his shoulder. Blood oozed from it. It did not look too dirty.

He had to make sure it stayed clean. He could not afford an infection, not when he was so close.

Opening up the bottle of iodine with his teeth, he poured a liberal amount onto another piece of gauze and dabbed at the wound, letting out a short hiss from the pain.

Don't be weak. God hates weakness in His vessels.

A regular thumping against the wall of the adjoining room reminded him just how weak some people could be. He wished he didn't have to hide in such a pit of sin, but at least this motel was anonymous.

The fornicators in the other room certainly appreciated that. They were probably cheating on their spouses, destroying the sanctity of holy matrimony.

The Chosen One felt tempted to go over there and punish them.

Stay on the path, he warned himself. *Do not get distracted by every sinner you meet, for you meet so many.*

The thumping increased in tempo. The Chosen One grimaced and focused on cleaning his wound.

He felt like wiping iodine on his entire body this place was so filthy. The bathtub had a yellow ring around the inside. The shower curtain was fringed with black mold. And on the edges of the sink, burns from crack pipes reminded him of those wasted years when places like this were his common haunt.

You have come far. You will go further.

Once the wound had been thoroughly disinfected, he put a piece of gauze over it and taped it to his skin. The sharp pain from the iodine reduced to a dull throb. He could live with that. He moved his arm around. While it hurt, he hadn't lost any movement or strength. He knew that if he exerted himself, it would start bleeding again, but there was nothing he could do about that. It was all in God's hands.

And God smiled on him. He was getting close. The gunshot was a warning for him to keep his faith and stay on the narrow path, but this also held the promise of victory and revelation. The Chosen One could rise to the status of an Apostle.

The sinners in the next room finally stopped making their racket.

Thank God for small mercies, he thought.

He fashioned a sling from the cloth in his First Aid kit and put his wounded arm in it. Best not to move it while he didn't need it.

Going into the bedroom, he looked at Little Peter propped up on the bed. His face glowed with a fresh coat of gold paint.

"Another sacrifice!" Little Peter said. "Yippie! And that means I get a coat of paint, making me as pure as God made me."

"That's right, Little Peter," the Chosen One said. "No one can touch you. No one can make you unclean."

With his good arm he opened a duffel bag, pulled out the three pieces of the Key, and laid them in a row on his bed.

First, the curled-up parchment from the ivory figurine at the Cloisters. On it, in Latin but written by a modern fountain pen were the words, "The first three squares: shortest, longest, widest hole."

Next, the Gorizia dodecahedron retrieved from the bust of Edward Gibbon in the Glencairn Museum.

Finally, a miniature gold set of calipers from the reliquary of St. Anselm at The Virginia Museum of Fine Arts, wrapped in buckskin so it wouldn't rattle in its hiding place and would remain hidden for all those years.

The calipers, he knew, were to measure certain edges of the Gorizia dodecahedron.

He felt sure that the parchment was telling him to measure certain dimensions of the dodecahedron, and that the shortest side, the longest side, and the widest hole would align to the first three squares on the cryptex that were part of the code to open it.

He still had to find a list of the other sides he needed to measure. Once he had that, he'd have everything.

And then he pulled out his most treasured possession, a diary written in the hand of Raymond Pitcairn, co-founder of the Glencairn Museum and one of the leading members of the Cryptex Club.

He had found it after diligent research and constant monitoring of the auction houses.

It was for sale among the papers of his secretary, Derrick Amberson. His name was not generally associated with Pitcairn's, having only worked for the millionaire for a couple of years. But the Chosen One's research showed that they had always kept in touch, and that Amberson continued to help his former employer through the years as sort of a secret assistant.

Amberson was better known as a historical novelist, writing novels with a Christian theme set in the Middle Ages. The papers that came up for auction included manuscripts for some of his novels as well as a diary that bore Amberson's name.

That piqued the Chosen One's interest, because another diary by Amberson, one covering the same years, had gone up for auction several years before.

When he examined the papers for sale, he found that the diary wasn't the late author's but in fact Pitcairn's.

He had to buy it. The Chosen One made a decent living as a licensed independent electrician, but nevertheless he had to dig deep into his savings.

It didn't matter. Worldly things meant nothing to him. And the diary contained exactly what he had prayed it would.

A list, in code, of each of the clues to the cryptex and in what objects they were hidden.

He had purchased that diary five years before, and only cracked the code last week.

Only to find that one of the objects he needed happened to be on loan from the Ashmolean Museum in Oxford to a show right here in the United States.

Happened to be? No. There by the grace of God.

But God made this another test for him, because that show would end in a week.

Hence his haste.

There was only one more piece of the key to retrieve. Once he had it, the clues would lead the way to the cryptex, and also give the instructions to unlock it.

The Chosen One checked his watch. Time for the morning news. Usually he didn't watch television, that fool's carnival of Godless debauchery, but he wanted to see how last night's events were being covered.

While his motel was on a state highway well away from Richmond, the room's cheap TV still carried Richmond's ABC affiliate.

When he turned it on, some harlot was selling shampoo, dancing around the shower and showing her bare shoulders, her body all but revealed through the foggy glass.

The Chosen One averted his eyes and slapped himself. The Devil had made him feel desire.

Weak. I am weak!

He put a towel over Little Peter's head and kept his own face to the wall, praying for his soul, until the commercial ended and switched to one for a local used car lot. The Chosen One kept praying.

The next commercial stuck the words in his throat.

"Summer is almost here, and it's time for children to have a vacation with Jesus. Holy Hills Bible Camp offers a summer of clean, spiritual fun set on a hundred acres of Virginia woodland."

The Chosen One whirled to glare at the television, which showed an idyllic lake surrounded by trees. Laughing children paddled a canoe. The scene switched to a prayer hall where adults led a group of children and teens in a worship service.

"Led by trained spiritual leaders, your child will learn to love the Lord while enjoying fresh air and sunshine."

Why are you crying? Doesn't Scripture say to love one another, to embrace your fellow Christian? Here, let's try something else you might like better ...

A shudder ran through the Chosen One's bulky frame, his rage soured by a lifelong feeling of disgust. He turned away, knowing that if he didn't, he'd kick in the TV screen.

And he needed to see the news. He needed to know what was going on.

Finally, the theme music for the news program came on.

He turned back to the TV.

A female announcer with far too much makeup but who at least had the decency to wear proper clothing gave her name and said,

"First up this morning, a deadly break-in at The Virginia Museum of Fine Arts that has left a security guard dead and a priceless work of art destroyed. Late last night, an unknown intruder disabled the alarm and security cameras and picked the lock to one of the staff entrances."

The reporter went through a basic narrative of the break in as pictures showed the outside of the museum, then closeups of the broken reliquary.

The reporter went on. "This medieval gold box—"

"Reliquary," the Chosen One corrected.

"—was broken open, the lid destroyed, and a bone purported to be from a medieval saint purposely destroyed."

"Thou shalt set up no idols before me!" the Chosen One screamed at the TV. "If he was truly a saintly man, he would not want his bones put in a flashy box of expensive materials!"

"Get thee behind me, Satan!" Little Peter said.

There was a thud on the wall. A voice, barely muffled by the cheap thin drywall, shouted. "Hey! Keep it down over there. We're trying to sleep."

The Chosen One grabbed his knife, glaring at the wall, wanting to kick right through it and slit those sinners' throats.

Control yourself. The Devil put them in your path to tempt you. You can't afford to draw any more attention to yourself than you absolutely have to.

"Stay on the path," Little Peter said.

Slowly, he sat back down to find he had missed an interview with the museum director, which was just finishing.

See how tricky the Devil can be?

He balled his hand into a fist, ready to hit his forehead as punishment, but not wanting to miss any more of the broadcast.

A ghostly image of himself appeared from the security footage before he could get to the electric panel controlling the camera and disable them.

"Police are looking for this man, who appears to be the same suspect responsible for the other two break-ins."

And the Devil stopped me from hearing about what they've figured out about those. Oh Lord, spare me from his evil ways!

The view cut to the outside of the museum, where several police cars were parked. Uniformed officers mingled with officers in white CSI suits and a few people in civilian clothes.

A familiar face made him leap forward and get within inches of the screen.

Professor Remi Laurent stood with the museum director and another man. He only saw her for a second, but he was sure.

"And now on to other news. The city government—"

The Chosen One flicked the TV off, pacing back and forth across the threadbare carpet.

She's here, studying the case.

Well of course she is. The police aren't stupid. They would have made the connection to the cryptex eventually. I'm surprised they made it so soon.

No, she must have made the connection. She's helping them.

The Chosen one froze mid-step. Was she an enemy or a friend? Sent by God or the Devil?

The police were certainly the tool of the Devil. Unwitting tools, to be sure, but that only made them more dangerous because they thought they were on the side of right. They saw the sacrifices as murders, saw his collecting the pieces of the key as theft.

And with Remi Laurent helping them, they were twice as dangerous.

What was her motivation? She wanted the cryptex as much as he did. He wasn't sure why, though. She always garlanded her articles in the high prose of academia, where no one professes their faith for fear of ridicule or censure.

Was she Godly, or did she want the cryptex thinking it would give her worldly gain?

No, she had always written of it as giving spiritual insight. Every one of her articles had made that clear.

So she might be a true seeker. Perhaps she was even using the police to get closer to him.

Yes! That must be it. That Godly woman knew he was close to finding all the keys to the cryptex. She was using the police's resources to figure out where he would strike next. Then she would mislead them and go to the right museum herself.

His heart thrilled at the thought. The Lord would soon reward him for the lonely path he had trodden. In His wisdom, He would provide His Chosen One with a woman who would help him find the cryptex and unlock its holy secrets. It would be a meeting of the minds, of the spirit.

And of the body.

Sanctified by the Lord.

Not the filth he was put through in the Bible camp all those years ago, but a holy union. It would wash all that filth away.

For a brief moment, the Chosen One felt that rarest of emotions for him—joy.

"Am I going to have a mommy?" Little Peter asked.

"Yes," the Chosen One said. "Yes, I think you will."

Soon he and Remi Laurent would meet, and he would make her his wife.

CHAPTER THIRTEEN

Daniel felt the case slipping through his fingers.

After their fumble with the last museum, they needed to get on track, trace the connections between the crime and figure out what the hell was going on.

The problem was that Daniel didn't see any connections.

He sat in his hotel room, staring at his note and the reports that had come in. Daniel and Remi had gotten adjoining motel rooms in Richmond since there was no point in returning to D.C. It would only waste time, and they didn't have much time.

The killer was in a hurry for some reason. Why else would he hit three museums in less than a week? That had started to draw nationwide attention. The ABC affiliate that had shown up at the museum had sent the story through the network. While CNN and Fox hadn't yet posted on it, several less popular websites had. It was on the verge of going viral.

That wouldn't have happened if the killer had bided his time, hit a museum once a year or so.

And with the clues hidden for a century in artifacts that never left their museums, why the rush?

So while the killer went on a whirlwind tour of medieval art collections, Daniel was stuck in a Motel 6 going through all the information the local police had gathered about the victims, their bosses, and coworkers. He was looking for connections and finding none.

He saw no evidence that the victims knew one another, knew Remi, or knew of the cryptex. Only one of the security guards, Ted Peterson, had any interest in medieval history, and even he didn't show any interest in or knowledge of the cryptex or anything related to it.

Same with the three museums. None had ever invited Remi to give a guest lecture, and none had ever hosted a talk or exhibition on the cryptex, cryptography, the occult, or anything remotely associated with this damn mythical artifact.

Mythical? God, he hoped not. That would mean all these people got sliced up for a shadow. At least let it be real, something actually worth trying to find.

Because if it wasn't, Remi would have wasted her entire career.

Even worse, her research into a myth would have kickstarted this whole killing spree.

The investigations from the local police departments investigating the various killings only added to the confusion—an avalanche of details of the crime scene and low-quality eyewitness reports from well-intentioned citizens who probably hadn't seen anything. He still had to trawl through it all, though.

Detective Fish's report from the Glencairn crime scene was the most useful. The CSI team had studied the boot print and came back with the results that it was a size 11 Timberland worn by a man who was about 210 lbs. Daniel dismissed this with a shrug. He had figured all that out from the first ten seconds of security camera footage.

Another item was far more interesting. In the clay that had flaked off the suspect's boot was a small fleck of gold paint. Chemical analysis showed it to be modern. There followed a long technical explanation about how gold is always mixed with other materials to make paint, and those materials have changed over time.

So the perp didn't have a flake of gold on his boot from smashing museum displays. He had it because he was painting something gold.

Oh, and the clay was modeler's clay.

Interesting. So this guy was not only a locksmith and electrician, but he had arts and crafts skills. Not to mention being versed in medieval history.

That was quite a broad range of talents for a complete nutcase. Daniel was beginning to suspect that this was the highest functioning serial killer he had ever dealt with.

It still didn't get him any closer to catching the guy.

While Daniel was getting nowhere with the usual lines of enquiry, Remi was in the next room going through all her history articles, trying to see what the killer saw through his eyes. He hoped she could find something.

Actually, he knew she would, given time.

But they didn't have time.

His phone rang. Daniel groaned, thinking it was Veronica.

The caller ID piqued his curiosity. It was his partner, Agent Nomellini.

Ex-partner, he reminded himself.

"Hey, Carmella. Any news?"

Agent Nomellini's friendly voice came over the line. "Hey Daniel. To quote a former president: 'Ladies and Gentlemen, we got him.'"

Daniel sat bolt upright. "Finger Man?"

"That's right, *compagno*."

"Where? How?"

She did it. Good for her!

"Where? In Jersey, where all scumbags live. How? Blind luck. He got pulled over by a patrol car for a routine stop. Broken taillight."

"No," Daniel gasped in stunned disbelief.

"Yep. When the cop asked him for his license and registration, he leapt out of the car with a knife. The cop took him down, beat him for a while like they do in Jersey, and cuffed him. Then he noticed dried blood on the knife. A search of the car found more bloodstains. They found the victims' fingers too. He had them tied to his own fingers, hidden inside an oversized pair of gloves."

Daniel nodded. "Tied to his own fingers to draw out the strength of those buff young men."

"Just like you said. And as you predicted, he's a shrimp. A scrawny older guy with a bald spot the size of Manhattan who couldn't bench press a plate of lasagna. Hated strong young men for having the vitality he lacked."

"So Finger Man is finished." Daniel could hardly believe it. He had felt certain that with him off the case and Nomellini not having any real help, the guy would get away with one or two more murders before he got caught.

But now fate had lent a hand.

"So how's your new life as a connoisseur of the arts?" his ex-partner asked.

Daniel let out a frustrated grunt. "This guy moves too fast. We don't have time to build up a proper profile."

He looked over at his computer and piles of paperwork, none of which, he felt sure, held the key to finding the perpetrator.

"You'll nab him. You always do."

"We always did," Daniel grumbled. *God, I wish she was on this case with me.*

"The *mammalucco* who transferred you deserves to have his fingers cut off and tied on the hands of some psycho. How can they break up the dynamic duo?"

"We solved a ton of murders," Daniel said, regret dripping from every word.

"And you'll solve a ton more. Grab yourself a beer. You deserve it. Hell, I deserve it. I think I'll go get one right now. And come over for dinner when you get the chance. The hellions are bugging me about you."

Agent Nomellini hung up.

Daniel lay back on the bed, not sure how to feel. Of course, he was happy the killer had been found. The blonde bodybuilders of America were safe once more. But the way the guy had been caught made Daniel feel kind of cheated. All that clever detective work and the guy panics at a traffic stop.

Well, just because he got away with eight murders doesn't mean he's intelligent.

The Cryptex Killer, on the other hand, that guy was intelligent, motivated, and skilled.

That made him ten times as dangerous as the finger-collecting freak who drove around New Jersey with a broken taillight.

His phone rang again.

Please don't let it be Veronica. She's the last person I want to talk to right now.

It turned out Daniel was wrong. The last person he wanted to talk to was Keiko Ochiai, head of the Antiquities Division. His "new boss."

"Agent Walker here." He tried to sound alert and professional, not exhausted from a sleepless night and bloated from pigging out at breakfast.

"How's the investigation progressing?" Assistant Director Ochiai asked in her Texas drawl. "You closing in on the suspect?"

Good morning to you too. Daniel glanced at his watch. *Oh crap, it's afternoon. 2pm already?*

"We're working on several leads."

"I need more than that. The media has figured out we're dealing with a serial killer. We don't need that sort of panic and notoriety. We need results."

"I've only been on the case a few days."

"The killer is on an accelerated schedule and you need to be too. Why were you at a different museum than the one that got hit last night?"

Daniel winced.

I knew you were going to ask that.

"Professor Laurent, who I mentioned in my last email report to you, suggested that one of the items the suspect is after would be hidden in a special exhibition in D.C."

"Was it?"

"Um, no."

"Are you sure this professor is a valuable asset?"

Daniel tried to be patient. "I explained that in my email. It's also good to have her close in order to protect her. I haven't spoken with her about this, because I don't want to frighten her, but our suspect is obviously an obsessive, and with Professor Laurent as the primary source of solid information on the cryptex, he's probably obsessed with her too."

"We can protect her if need be. What I'm worried about is that her advice may not be as helpful as you think it is."

"She's helped a great deal with—"

"She steered you to the wrong museum and someone ended up killed. She needs to do better. *You* need to do better. I accepted you in the Antiquities Division because of your background. Please don't make me regret that decision. Now I'll let you get back to work. Send me another update tonight."

She hung up.

"A goodbye would have been nice," Daniel grumbled.

That goodbye might come later in the form of a pink slip.

Daniel had spent his career analyzing other people, and he could recognize a stressed-out boss issuing a veiled threat when he saw one. Assistant Director Ochiai had started a new division, one that was an odd fit for the agency, and her first big case was leaving a trail of blood and bad publicity across the northeastern states.

And what was her turn of phrase? "I accepted you in the Antiquities Division." Not requested. Accepted. Daniel had been handed off like some secondhand clothing to Goodwill. Damaged goods for the oddball new division.

Assistant Director Ochiai hadn't wanted him on her team. Given his list of infractions, she probably felt it was an insult to have to take him.

Daniel tossed his phone on the bed, then tossed himself on the bed too. He lay there for a minute, staring at the ceiling and wishing he was anywhere else.

He'd missed the chance to solve the Finger Man case, and now his new boss was chewing him out for not pulling the Cryptex Killer out of a hat.

Daniel looked ahead at his future in the FBI and did not see much. If Assistant Director Ochiai kicked him out of the Antiquities Division, there was no way in hell he'd get back into the Behavioral Affairs Unit. He'd be lucky if he got stuck doing legwork for some two-bit bureau in one of the flyover states.

His real talents would be wasted, and more people would die at the hands of killers only he could catch.

A knock on the door.

If that's another guy here to serve me papers, I'm going to cut his damn fingers off and make a glove out of them.

Daniel got up, looked through the spyhole, and saw Remi standing on the other side. Even through the distorted lens of the peephole he could see she looked as tired as he felt. He opened the door.

"Please tell me you have something," he grumbled.

"I might," Remi replied, sounding a bit irritated at his tone. Well, tough nuts. He was irritated too.

She came in, laptop in hand and already open. Seeing the motel room's undersized desk was already covered with papers and his own laptop, she set her computer down on the bed.

The screen showed a map of the United States with markers at various cities.

"I've gone through my research and pulled out the locations of every medieval item from the collections of the Cryptex Club. Now some are in private collections and I don't know where those are, but I believe those items would not contain clues to the cryptex. In their wills, the members stipulated which items should go into museums and which could be kept by their heirs or sold. This is a map of where the rest of the items are held."

Daniel looked at the map and despaired. "There's got to be a dozen points on here."

"Seventeen," Remi said, a note of apology in her voice, "Including items in two German museums and an English one."

"Jesus Christ," Daniel muttered.

"Look, all we have to do is call the local police departments in all these cities. We put the museums on alert and post policemen at every institution."

Daniel sighed. Civilians never understood. "So you want me to call up the police forces of seventeen different cities—"

"Fourteen. The killer has already struck at three of these places."

"Fourteen different cities and tell them to lock down their biggest museums and post men desperately needed elsewhere in these museums all night. And for how many nights?"

Remi raised her hands, utterly baffled.

"Why not?"

"Why not? Because they won't do it, that's why not," Daniel said, his irritation rising. "We might be able to get the museums to close for a few days. Might. But we don't have the authority to make them do that and it probably won't help anyway, given this guy's skill set. And there's no way all these police departments are going to pull men to sit in a museum all night. You saw the trouble we had in D.C. It will be the same everywhere, or worse. Every police department I know is overstretched. They're not going to use up at least two men for an entire night shift on a hunch."

Remi frowned. "It is not a hunch. He will certainly strike one of these places."

"You're casting your net too wide. This isn't a plan, it's a start of a plan. Do you have any insight into which museums are more likely?"

"No," Remi said in a quiet voice. "I'm working on it."

Daniel saw he had hurt her and softened his tone. "You go do that. And send me this list. I'll get to work notifying everyone. We can at least put them on their guard."

She nodded, obviously worn out.

Daniel felt bad. This civilian had been thrown head-first into the deep end and he had snapped at her just because his boss had snapped at him.

"You're doing good," he said. She looked up at him. "Seriously. I've worked with a lot of civilian advisors and you've put in more effort than any three put together."

She managed a weak smile and stood.

"All right. I'll try to narrow it down," she said as she left his motel room.

You better, Daniel thought. *Because I'm all out of ideas and if you don't come up with something, before long there's going to be another broken artifact, and another dead body.*

CHAPTER FOURTEEN

Remi huffed back to her room, irritated in the extreme. This man bursts into her lecture, yanks her out of her life, and drags her all over the place looking at crime scenes, and doesn't even listen to her?

Why couldn't the police guard every museum? It would only take a couple of officers from each jurisdiction.

Oh, because her idea was only a "hunch." He wanted results, and he wanted them now.

And that half-hearted apology tacked onto the end of his rudeness was only to motivate her to work harder, as if becoming one of the world's leading historians had been accomplished without motivation.

Policemen. She knew all their tricks.

Daniel reminded her of her own father. He'd been an officer in the Police Nationale in Paris. He worked the same long hours as Daniel, and was the same overeating, overbearing, and overworked ball of stress as the FBI agent.

He died of a heart attack at age 53, dropping to the pavement as he chased down a gang member who had just slashed a rival's face with a razor.

Leaving Remi without a father she never really had.

Daniel hadn't mentioned a wife or children. That was probably for the best. If a man wanted to be an obsessive loner, he shouldn't burden other people with that.

Remi returned to her room to find her phone, which she had left on her desk, buzzing. The screen indicated it was Cyril.

She rushed to grab it just as Cyril hung up.

"*Merde,*" Remi muttered. She was old enough to remember a life before mobile phones. It had been more peaceful. She returned his call.

"Hey, where are you? Are you alright?" her boyfriend asked.

"Yes. No. I don't know. I'm in Richmond. We're tracking down the killer."

"I saw the news about the murder. Were you there?" The worry in his voice was endearing. Remi wanted to kiss him through the phone.

“No, we were … checking out another lead.” Remi didn’t want to admit the mistake she had made.

“Thank God you didn’t cross his path. The dean got a call from the FBI today. Said all your classes were canceled until further notice. You haven’t been hired by the FBI, have you?”

He sounded incredulous, and perhaps a bit jealous. That struck Remi as funny. She held the phone away from her head for a second as she suppressed a giggle.

“Not exactly,” she replied. “I’m acting as a consultant. Since I’m the world’s leading cryptex researcher, they need me to figure out the killer’s movements.”

Cyril muttered something she couldn’t catch. She thought it sounded like, “Well at least it’s good for something.” Remi glared at the phone. In a more audible voice he said, “I’m worried about you. I don’t want you to cross paths with that maniac. Should I come down?”

Remi blinked. She had expected him to say that she should drop the case, but of course he wouldn’t do that. He knew how dedicated she was. So instead, he wanted to put himself in harm’s way. For her.

“Thank you for the offer, but I don’t think he’ll want you along,” Remi said with a smile.

“Who’s he?”

Despite her stress and exhaustion, Remi almost laughed at the flagrant jealousy she heard in that question.

“Agent Walker, a very rude FBI man who eats bacon double cheeseburgers for breakfast.”

“Sounds like a barbarian.”

“He is a barbarian. But he’s devoted, and I think with my help we’ll be able to catch this killer.”

“Good. Just don’t let him put you in harm’s way.”

“Last night he refused to let me stay on a stakeout he was doing,” Remi told him, deciding to leave out how she had responded to that.

“Good. Do you think you’ll be back tomorrow?”

“I don’t know. I don’t think so.”

“Well, how long is he going to keep you?”

“Until we catch the murderer, I suppose.”

“What? Why can’t you advise him from home? Skip your lectures if you need to, but at least you’ll be out of harm’s way.”

With this man studying all my research, I don't think I'll be out of harm's way until he's caught, Remi thought, pacing around the cramped motel room.

She didn't want to tell Cyril that. He'd get even more worried.

"I need to be at the scene, looking at the artifacts. It's the only way I can get inside this killer's mind."

Pause. "Wait. You want to grab those clues for yourself!"

Remi blushed. On several occasions she had enthused over dinner about how she wanted to find the clues the Cryptex Club had hidden and discover the secret of the fabled device herself. She had always thought his eyes had glazed over during these conversations. Now it looked like he had paid more attention than she realized.

"He knows something I've missed. Maybe he discovered another piece of evidence. I need to find that."

"You need to stay out of the way of a maniacal killer. This isn't some research project, Remi. This guy has killed three people already."

"Yes, but—"

"Look. You know I think you'd be better off focusing more mainstream subjects. You'd get more respect from your colleagues. Look how well your papers on incunables, later period feudalism, and medieval trade routes have been received. And now you want to bring up this? If they hear you're hunting after the same thing as this serial murderer, they'll think you're some fringy nut working at a community college."

A memory rose up from Remi's subconscious, something from a conference several years ago.

"What did you say?" Remi gasped.

Misreading her response, Cyril was quick to go on. "I'm not saying you *are* a fringy nut. You're a serious researcher. But perception is important in this discipline. You—"

"I have to go," Remi said.

"Wait. Don't be mad. I—"

"I'm not mad. I think you might have just solved the case!"

She hung up, already running for Daniel's room and pounding on his door.

Daniel opened up, phone in hand. "Look, sorry about snapping at you. I've been talking to the local PDs and—"

"Never mind about that. I think I know the murderer!"

Daniel cocked his head. "What, personally?"

"I think I met him at a conference several years ago." Remi glanced over as an elderly tourist couple came down the hallway, rolling their suitcase behind them. "Let me in."

Daniel grinned. "Right. Let's not frighten the civilians."

Remi figured that was supposed to be a compliment, but she was in too much of a hurry to tell him her theory. She pushed past him and started pacing back and forth in his room.

"I had pushed this man out of my mind because he was a fool, but I think he was less of a fool than I first thought."

"Who?" Daniel asked, standing in a corner since that was all the room Remi allowed him.

"Andrew. Andrew something. He taught history at a community college somewhere. I'll remember in a minute. Maryland. Right! Baltimore City Community College."

Daniel started tapping away on his phone.

"Pay attention," Remi snapped. "He—"

"Don't talk to me like one of your students. I'm looking this guy up."

"Oh. Anyway. I was at a conference in New York City hosted by the Met, and he was in attendance. I remember him. Thin, wild eyed. He had written a paper on medieval occultism that he wanted to present at the conference, but they didn't accept it. Probably because it didn't pass peer review. I remember he gave it to me, and I couldn't get past the first page. Conferences always attract a few fringe types. So Andrew—"

"Andrew Critchfield?" Daniel asked, holding up his phone and showing her a staff photo of the man she remembered. He still had the long, gaunt features, the bugging blue eyes, and the stringy, poorly kept brown curls down to his shoulders. He looked like a hippy on a bad trip. Remi got the impression he had always looked like that.

"Right! That's him. Is he still at the same place?"

"Yes."

"Good. So Andrew cornered me during one of the meet and greet sessions and started telling me all about the cryptex. He knew more than I thought he would, but his interpretations were all wrong. He believed in occultism, thought medieval magic was real. He even claimed to be a magician himself. I must admit I stopped listening at that point. I do remember one thing, though. He claimed he knew the location of the cryptex. He felt dead sure it was hidden in Christ Church Cathedral in Hartford, Connecticut."

"Do you remember where in the cathedral?"

Remi stopped pacing.

She opened her mouth. That crazed man had told her, and it had seemed so unlikely that she had dismissed the idea out of hand. Now, after all that had happened, she wasn't so sure.

But if she told Daniel, he might try to leave her behind. Even worse, he might inform the cathedral, they might retrieve the cryptex themselves, and she wouldn't get to see it at all.

"I don't remember. I'm not sure he told me. I'll have to have a look around for myself."

Did she see disbelief in Daniel's eyes, or only the reflection of her own guilt? She felt bad for lying to this man, who, as irritating as he could be, put his life in danger to help strangers.

But she had to see for herself. She had to *know*.

"Anything else you can remember about this guy?" Daniel asked.

"Not much, I'm afraid. I recall I acted a bit dismissively. I've been cornered by this sort of people too many times to count. He got angry, forceful. Insisted that he was correct in his theories. And … oh." A chill ran through her as another detail of that old, half-remembered conversation came back to her. "He said that if it turned out he was wrong, or he was right, he would get in touch."

"Has he?"

"No, but … what if he is in another way? What if he's contacting me through these murders, by using my research to track down the clues to the cryptex's location?"

Daniel tapped the thumb of his right hand against his thigh. Remi had seen him do that before when his interest was aroused. She wondered if he even knew he did it.

Now that Remi was no longer pacing, he could move over to his desk, where he opened his laptop and ran a search for Andrew Critchfield. Remi leaned over his shoulder to look more closely at the screen. Daniel's breath still stank of the onions from that breakfast burger, but Remi was too intrigued to care much.

Besides a staff profile for Baltimore City Community College, there was a private Facebook account and several articles on the cryptex on the kinds of fringe websites she never visited.

Daniel refined the search to include both Andrew Critchfield's name and her own.

Remi stood up straight, taking in a quick intake of breath. Google brought up several hits.

One was for the conference they had both attended. The rest were citations of her work in his online articles.

Daniel pulled out his phone. "I'm calling this guy."

"Do you think that's wise? Won't it alert him?"

"I'm going to pretend to be a reporter and ask about the cryptex. Loser loners like this can't resist talking about their pet theories."

"How do you know he's a loner?"

"So few hits on Google. No mention of family or activities, no photos beyond that staff pic, and I'll bet you a hundred bucks the friends on that Facebook page are all weirdos like him. I've seen this a million times."

Daniel dialed Critchfield's office number. It rang and rang. The FBI agent did not look surprised and busied himself with looking up the department number.

When he called that number, he didn't pretend to be a reporter, but instead identified himself as an agent of the FBI.

Remi began pacing again, listening in to one half of the conversation.

Half was all she needed.

"Really? Not for four days? Have you tried his home number? Not answering? Thank you, ma'am. If he gets in touch or shows up at work, please call me. Yes, right away. No, don't tell him anything. That's right. Goodbye."

Daniel hung up and turned to her. She stopped pacing.

"Hasn't been to work in four days and isn't answering calls or emails."

"He disappeared just when the break-ins started," Remi said, feeling a bit faint.

"Bingo. They gave me his cell number. I'm going to have the techy folks at the agency track him."

"Will that take long?"

"Not at all."

"Don't you need a warrant for that?"

"Theoretically," Daniel said with a wink. "In reality? Big Brother is watching you."

How often does this man break the law in order to enforce it?

To her surprise, Remi discovered she didn't care all that much, certainly not in this situation.

"Will this take long?" she asked.

"Just a few minutes."

"I'll go pack," Remi said.

Remi returned to her room and hurriedly threw her clothes and other things into her bag, her mind racing.

The altar. He said the cryptex was hidden in the altar. A church couldn't be any more difficult to break into than a museum, so has he already retrieved it? Or no, maybe he wanted to get the clues first. The cryptex is no good without them. I wish I knew how many clues there were. It would give me an idea how close he was. Nobody's knows that, though. Unless he does.

Once packed, she ran back to Daniel's room and tried to enter without knocking, only to find the door locked.

He's cautious. I guess it's natural considering his job. Perhaps I should take a lesson from that.

Daniel must have heard her try the door because he opened it, cocked his head, and gave her an approving smile.

"Looks like we're going to Hartford."

CHAPTER FIFTEEN

Daniel checked his messages as they got off their flight at Hartford-Bradley airport and found one from Veronica that he skipped, and two from other people that he read.

The first was from the Hartford PD saying they had a squad car waiting for them at the airport. The second was from Wayne, his friend at the FBI phone tracing unit. A bit of a geek, but he believed in catching bad guys more than he believed in following the strict letter of the law. That made him a hero in Daniel's eyes. He'd been tracking the phone and said it was still in the same location it had been for the last few hours, a Howard Johnson's downtown.

They rushed out of the terminal and straight to the waiting patrol car. Daniel grimaced when he saw the Hartford PD had only given them one cop, but the man told them they could call for backup if need be. Daniel was in such a hurry he didn't even get the guy's name.

The twenty-minute drive to the hotel felt like an hour. Daniel sent a message to Wayne asking if the location had changed.

He got a message back within a minute.

"Of course not. You think I'm an idiot? I would have told you."

A bit prickly. Just like Remi. Don't question a specialist's specialty. I should remember that.

The squad car pulled up just around the corner from the hotel to reduce the chance that the suspect might see them, and they proceeded on foot.

A glance at the officer's uniform took care of the woman at the front desk, who looked up Andrew Critchfield and told them he was in Room 322. Daniel and Remi took the stairs while the cop took the elevator, just in case the guy came down at that moment.

They met outside the room, the officer taking one side of the door and Daniel on the other so the suspect couldn't look out the peephole and see them. He had left Remi by the door to the stairs. She peeked around the doorway and Daniel irritably motioned for her to get out of sight.

Jesus. Doesn't she know some civilians carry guns in this country?

Once the professor was safely out of sight, Daniel squared his shoulders and took a deep breath.

Time to get this done.

The officer made eye contact with Daniel and made a motion of knocking.

Daniel shook his head, pulled out his gun, and kicked the door in.

He rushed in, 9mm leveled, the cop right behind.

No one in the room. Daniel dove to the side, expecting a shot from the bathroom. The cop came right beside him.

"Andrew Critchfield, this is the FBI. Come out with your hands up!"

Silence.

Damn it. Wish we had some tear gas.

Daniel took a quick look and ducked back. He didn't see anyone.

"Final warning!"

Daniel counted to ten, heart beating fast.

If I get shot in the line of duty, Veronica will nag at me the rest of my life.

Focus.

He burst into the bathroom, leading with his gun.

No one.

"Crap, he's not here," Daniel said.

The cop gestured at the bedside table. "His phone is."

"He knows we might be looking for him," Daniel said. "We got to find this guy."

"Let's go to the cathedral," Remi said.

Daniel spun around. The professor stood at the doorway.

"Didn't I tell you to wait at the stairs?" Daniel bellowed.

"He's not here, you just said so."

"Yeah, like three seconds ago."

"Jesus Christ, why can't you listen. I—"

Rem cocked her head. "Are you going to lecture me, or are we going to get to the cathedral before he stabs somebody?"

"Quiet," Daniel barked.

He didn't bother to listen to her response, which was in French anyway and no doubt obscene. Instead, he did a quick survey of the room—luggage, clothing, toiletries. Nothing else. None of the stolen items. No weapons.

"We need to get going," Remi said.

"Right," Daniel grumbled, rushing out of the room with the cop. Remi just barely managed to get out of the way in time. Too bad. She deserved to get run over.

On the trip downtown, the cop called for backup but wisely did not turn on his siren. If Critchfield really was at Christ Church Cathedral, warning him might make him panic, and you did not want a panicked nutcase.

But would he be there? Nighttime break-ins were his style. Safer too. There would be people at this place. Maybe he was scoping it out before planning to break in tonight.

But wait. Part of his thing was to kill someone after he found a piece of the puzzle. Cathedrals generally did not have night watchmen.

So if he wanted to kill someone, he'd have to do it in the daytime.

Crap.

"How much backup are they sending?" Daniel asked.

"One squad car."

"Get three."

"I'm not sure—"

"Get three!" Daniel snapped.

The officer got on the radio.

Daniel glanced in the rearview mirror at Remi and saw she had that faraway look, lips moving soundlessly. Lost in thought in that weird way of hers. Good. Maybe she could think of where else Critchfield might be if a search of the cathedral turned up nothing.

"With the traffic like it is, we'll be about ten minutes," the cop said between calls on the radio.

"Have the other units stand by out of sight but don't move in on the cathedral," Daniel told him.

While the police officer continued to talk on the radio, Daniel used his phone to pull up Christ Church Cathedral on Google street view to check out the area.

The cathedral was an old neo-Gothic brownstone tucked between modern glass office buildings. It looked like it had been modelled on the country churches of England.

He'd been to plenty of those, on one of his last trips to Europe with his mom and "Uncle" Ray …

Mom and Uncle Ray had been fighting again. They'd been dating for three years, Daniel was thirteen now, and the fights had started a few months before.

They never fought in front of him, but he could feel the tension. Mom was growing distant, both from him and Ray, and Daniel knew she wouldn't pay attention to the things he still didn't have the courage to tell her.

So while Mom was busy at a museum in Cambridge, Ray drove Daniel in a rented car through the Cambridgeshire and Essex countryside, looking at the castles Daniel liked, and the churches Daniel hated.

He hated them because it was Ray's favorite place to do it.

So his heart sank and he grew sullen as they pulled up at an isolated neo-Gothic country church. Gray stone under a gray sky. Mossy tombstones in an overgrown churchyard. A small town a couple of miles down the lane. A Tuesday morning. Daniel knew it would be empty.

So did Ray.

They parked. Daniel crossed his arms.

"I hate this," he muttered, his voice barely audible.

"You don't hate that model airplane I bought you yesterday," Ray said.

Daniel said nothing.

"You don't hate this either," Ray said, laughing off his objection. "You used to think it was exciting. Rebellious. I don't know what's gotten into you lately."

"I never liked it."

"Don't be silly."

"I want a girlfriend," Daniel said, looking out the window.

"This is practice for a girlfriend. You want to know what to do with her, don't you?"

"I'm sick of it," Daniel said, again almost too quiet to hear.

But Ray heard. He always heard.

"You sound like your mother."

Daniel grimaced. That was the worst part, sharing this guy with Mom.

He knew all he had to do was tell Mom and it would be all over. Or tell a teacher. Or a policeman. Dad had been a policeman until that druggie shot him. If Dad was alive, he'd shoot Ray.

All he had to do was tell.

But what would he tell them? Everything he and Ray did? And when they asked how long it had been going on, what could he say?

Two years? They'd ask why he hadn't told before. They might even laugh at him and say he liked it, the same as Ray always did.

And what if word got around? What if the kids at school found out?

"Just a few minutes," Ray said. "I promise. And nothing you don't like."

Daniel didn't like any of it, but Ray wouldn't believe that. After objecting strongly enough he'd managed to stop some things, the worst things. But that was it. Ray couldn't be put off from everything.

Ray smiled and looked up at the tower through the windshield. "This looks like an interesting church. Pevsner writes about it. Bring his book."

As Ray turned his back to get out of the car, Daniel gave him the finger. Then he retrieved the architectural guidebook from the glove compartment and got out too.

There was no point arguing. On these long European trips, he was far, far away from all his friends. He didn't have the strength to argue with the only person who paid attention to him.

A poke in the shoulder woke him out of his reverie.

"Hey, are you alright?" Remi asked. It sounded like she had asked that a couple of times already.

A sidelong glance from the cop driving the car confirmed it.

"Yeah, um. Just thinking. Zoned out a bit there. We at the cathedral yet?"

"Almost."

"Good. Let's shoot this piece of trash."

Another sidelong look from the police officer. "You mean arrest?"

"Right. Figure of speech."

They pulled up in front of a theater. The cathedral stood on a corner half a block down the street.

"The other units are all in position," the officer said. "Holding back just like you asked.

"Put a man on that side door," Daniel ordered, pointing. "Then come with us to the main entrance. You stay out of sight just to the side of the entrance while we go in."

The cop looked in the rearview mirror at Remi. "With the civilian?"

"We need her eyes. You study that photo of Andrew Critchfield?"

"Yes," the police officer said. "So I'm not really sure why the civilian needs to come in."

Daniel took a deep breath. He had Remi second guessing him all the damn time, he didn't need it from some local beat cop.

"She's the expert consultant on the case, plus she personally knows the perp and we don't. She'll hang back."

This last was said while glaring at Remi in the rearview mirror. She nodded.

God, she's annoying. But the fact of the matter is, I'm beginning to want to find this cryptex thing almost as much as she does. If I could grab the killer AND find some priceless artifact, maybe the FBI will be happy enough to transfer me back to BAU.

"You sure you can recognize the suspect?" Daniel asked the officer again.

"Yes."

"Good. Let's roll," Daniel said, checking his gun.

* * *

Remi felt lightheaded as they got out of the squad car. All her questions might be answered in the next few minutes. In a dreamlike state, she walked with the two men down the block. A policeman jogged out of a nearby office building and stood by a side entrance to the church.

They came around the corner and within view of the front entrance.

"*Merde*," Remi said.

A group of grade schoolers was just going inside.

"Should we hold off?" the police officer asked.

Daniel paused, then shook his head. "No. We can't leave that psycho inside with those kids."

"It might be more dangerous for them if we confront him," the policeman objected.

"It will be a hell of a lot worse to leave them helpless in there!" Daniel snapped.

The officer took half a step back. "Your call."

They walked over to the entrance, the policeman stopping just short of it. Remi and Daniel trailed in behind a teacher who was herding the last of her charges into the church.

As they entered the church, Remi scanned the spacious interior over the heads of the children, their happy chatter echoing up to the vaulted ceiling high overhead. A long nave stretched about forty meters to an altar. The interior was lit by bright sunlight coming through stained glass windows. Besides the school group, a few people prayed at the pews and several tourists wandered around taking pictures and admiring the artwork.

No one stood near the altar except for an African American couple, and in her first look around Remi did not see the community college professor she had met all those years ago.

Then she noticed a man in a jean jacket and baseball cap sitting in one of the front pews. He sat right next to the aisle, hunched over a bit as if to make himself less visible.

Remi turned to say something and saw Daniel had already noticed him.

He led her a little down the aisle and to the side.

"That could be him," he said in a low voice. "I don't see him anywhere else."

"We haven't checked the side chapels," Remi said.

"Let me check this guy out first. Stay here."

Daniel moved slowly down the aisle, shifting a bit to keep tourists in between him and the seated man as much as possible. The man did not turn around, his attention seemingly fixated on the altar.

One altar. What about the side chapels? Remi wondered.

She moved to the right and along the edge of the nave, casting nervous glances at Daniel as he closed the distance between himself and the man in the cap. She passed an old woman praying loudly to herself and ducked into the side chapel.

And stopped.

Only one person was in the side chapel, half obscured as he crouched behind the altar.

Remi must have made a sound, because the man looked up.

Andrew Critchfield looked right at her.

His eyes sparked with recognition.

CHAPTER SIXTEEN

Remi's heart raced. The community college professor stood barely ten meters from her, giving her a defiant sneer.

"Professor Laurent. I guess I shouldn't be surprised."

Remi, tense, resisted the urge to back away. She remembered summers in Provence as a child on her grandparents' farm, and being told if one of the neighborhood dogs growled at her to stand her ground and not show fear.

Andrew Critchfield shook his head. "I have to admit I got you wrong. I thought you were just some ivory tower bookworm. Turns out you're a nut."

"Me?"

A nobody teacher working at some nowhere community college calling one of the world's leading medievalists a nut? The nerve!

But don't the insane always think everyone else is mad?

Remi didn't move. She resisted the urge to look over her shoulder to look for Daniel. Hopefully he'd get over here before Critchfield tried anything.

Curiosity overcame her fear and, swallowing hard, she asked, "Did you find it? You said it was in the altar, but you meant the altar of the side chapel, not the main altar."

Critchfield puffed out with pride. "The main altar was consecrated in 1829. This is the Chapel of the Nativity. The guidebooks tell you it was consecrated in 1907, and that's true. What they don't tell you is that it was remodeled in 1932."

"Just the right period," Remi whispered.

She looked around for the first time, glancing back at Critchfield every couple of seconds to make sure he didn't try anything.

It was a cozy, warm room of wood paneling and a blue ceiling decorated with stars. It seemed designed as a place for quiet reflection, away from the crowds of the main cathedral.

And Remi felt excruciatingly aware that they were all alone here.

Critchfield smiled and stepped out from behind the altar. He had nothing in his hands, neither a knife nor the cryptex. Remi felt both relief and a crushing disappointment. Could she have been wrong?

"Where is it?" he demanded.

"I-I just asked you that," she stammered, wanting to run but not quite managing to get her legs moving. Instead, she fidgeted, shifting her weight from one leg to the other.

"You took it," he growled, moving forward another few steps and causing Remi to creep back toward the doorway. "You stole my research and now you've stolen the cryptex."

"Wait, if I did that, why would I be here?"

Critchfield's face reddened, his bugged eyes growing fierce. "To gloat! You think you're so smart, with your rich girl education and your visiting grants. All those publications, all those guest lectures, based on *my* research!"

"I've never even read any of your papers!"

As soon as the words came out of her mouth, Remi realized she had said the wrong thing. Critchfield snarled, hands balled into fists, and stalked toward her. He was thin, with an unhealthy pallor, but still youthful and he looked full of energy.

The community college teacher's voice rose to a screech that echoed through the cathedral. "You bitch. You deny it? You stole everything from me!"

Remi fumbled in her purse for her pepper spray, knowing she'd never get it in time as he rushed her.

"What you got in there?" Critchfield demanded, grabbing her purse. "You got the cryptex? You want to wave it in front of my face?"

He rummaged through the purse tossing the contents out, then threw it spitefully on the floor.

"Where is it?" He shrieked.

A blur from the left. Daniel tackled Critchfield around the midsection and they both went down. The community college teacher let out a loud grunt as he hit hard against the tiles.

Daniel ended up on top of him. He slugged the younger man, then flipped him over, fumbling for the handcuffs on the right side of his belt.

"Crap! Hurt my elbow going down," he grumbled.

Remi could see he wasn't using his right arm at all.

She moved toward them to help, then hesitated.

Critchfield thrashed around, trying to get Daniel off him. A couple more slugs from Daniel with his left hand calmed him down.

Remi plucked up the courage to duck down, pull the cuffs out of their holder, and hand them to him.

Then she darted back out of reach before Critchfield could try anything.

Daniel flipped him over and cuffed him, taking extra time since he still wasn't using his right arm very well.

"Go get that officer at the front door," he said.

Remi hesitated. "Are you alright?"

Daniel stood, grimacing as he flexed his arm. "I will be in a minute. Nothing broken."

Remi pushed through the crowd of staring tourists and wide-eyed schoolchildren that now blocked the entrance to the chapel and hurried for the main entrance. She noticed a couple of them snapping her picture.

This case is beginning to get notoriety. The news outlets are picking it up. I hope some reporter doesn't come around asking me questions.

She fetched the police officer, who dispersed the crowd as Daniel led the handcuffed community college teacher out of the cathedral. More people snapped pictures. Remi realized that if any of these got put on the Internet and linked to the case, her name would end up in the headlines.

It will pass, she told herself. *The average American TV watcher can't pay attention to more than one story at a time. As soon as some celebrity goes into rehab or a senator gets caught with a prostitute, this case will be out of the news and I can go back to my normal life. We have him now. It's over.*

Right?

* * *

Daniel and a local homicide detective named Gavers sat in the interrogation room at the Hartford downtown police station with Andrew Critchfield. Gavers was a tough-looking, solid man in his middle age who had the body of someone ten years younger. Hartford had a high crime rate and this guy looked like he had seen a lot of it.

The room was almost identical to the one where he had interviewed that idiot security guard. Most interrogation rooms were interchangeable—the same blank walls, the same lowlife handcuffed to a chair, the same undrinkable coffee. The only difference was that actually had the right guy this time.

Remi stood on the other side of the one way glass, watching the proceedings and listening through a microphone.

Daniel and Gavers sat opposite Critchfield as he fidgeted in his chair, one leg jerking up and down, making the handcuffs rubs against the edge of the chair with an annoying scrape of metal on plastic. He'd calmed down a bit once Remi got out of sight. Just a bit.

"So tell us again why you were in Christ Church Cathedral," Daniel said. He'd heard it all in the squad car coming to the station, but Critchfield had been ranting so much Daniel couldn't keep it all straight.

I should spend more time with normal people. It might do me some good.

Critchfield let out a low growl from deep in his throat. For a second Daniel thought he was going to launch into another tirade. Instead, his voice came out harsh and angry, yet level.

"Searching for the cryptex. I thought the Cryptex Club had hidden the device in the Chapel of the Nativity during its remodel."

"The Cryptex Club?" Detective Gavers asked.

Critchfield's face reddened. "Ask that bitch about it! I'm sure she's been telling you all about it! Stealing my research to make a nice comfy career for herself!"

"Whoa, calm down there, Andrew," Daniel said. "Tel us why you thought the cryptex was hidden in the chapel."

Critchfield ground his teeth, casting enraged glances at the one-way glass behind which he no doubt guessed Remi stood watching. After a minute, he spoke.

"The architect who remodeled the chapel had worked for a couple of the club members, so I thought there was a link. Also because of the star pattern on the ceiling. There's evidence linking medieval astrologers to the cryptex."

Critchfield paused, hanging his head. Detective Gavers cut in.

"We searched your hotel room and vehicle and didn't find this device you mention. We also searched both altars of the cathedral and didn't find any hidden compartments. Are you saying it's buried under the cathedral floor or something?"

The community college teacher slumped further, his chin almost touching his chest. When next he spoke, his voice came out as a whisper.

"No. It isn't there. I was wrong."

"Where is it then?" Detective Gavers asked.

Critchfield shook his head.

"Where's the cryptex, Andrew?" Daniel asked.

"I don't know. I was wrong. It wasn't buried there."

"So where have you been the last four days?" Daniel asked. "You've skipped your classes, you haven't been answering your phone, and you're a long way from Baltimore."

"When I read about the break-in at the Cloisters, I immediately knew the significance. The Cloisters were brought over from France by members of the Cryptex Club, and when I heard about the ivory figurine being broken, I knew someone was after the clues. Figurines like that had holes drilled in them when they were made so they could be fitted on dowels. I figured a parchment or something had been rolled up and hidden inside. That's why the intruder broke it."

"Where's the parchment, Andrew?" Daniel asked, throat going dry with anticipation. Now that they had the perp, getting the cryptex seemed enticingly close.

"I don't know. Why would I have it?"

"Come on, Andrew. You've been missing for four days. You're an expert on this stuff. You have a grudge against Professor Laurent. You tried to get violent with her."

"I was only shouting at her." Critchfield looked worried now. He had stopped accusing her of stealing the cryptex some time ago, his unstable mind slowly coming around to his unpleasant reality.

"We pulled your record," Detective Gavers said. "Twice you got pulled in for fights. Once with a neighbor in your apartment complex, and once with someone at a supermarket."

"They started it!"

"It takes two to have a fight, Andrew," Daniel said. "I read those reports. Both started with verbal altercations, and in both cases you were the first to swing."

Daniel had also read that Andrew had gotten the worst end of each fight. Was that why he resorted to sneaking up on people with knives?

"We also pulled your record at Baltimore City Community College," Detective Gavers said. "Your department chair wrote you up three times for screaming at students—"

"Bunch of entitled brats. They don't respect history!"

Daniel suppressed a smile. He knew a certain French professor who would agree with that.

"So where have you been for the past four days?" Daniel asked.

His buddy at the FBI had been able to ping Andrew's phone since it was an emergency but getting the records of his phone's movements would require a search of the phone company's records, and that really would require a warrant. The judge would grant it, of course, but that would take time. Daniel wanted his answers now, and then corroborate them with the actual records.

Briefly he wondered when that warrant to search JSTOR's database would come through. An agent at the New York office had already agreed to oversee the search at JSTOR's office once the warrant came through.

"So where have you been, Andrew?" Detective Gavers asked.

The community college teacher finally answered.

"Going around the museums where I thought the killer might go. Baltimore, Syracuse, Philadelphia. Here. I came here first, right after checking out the art museum in Baltimore. I searched both altars in the cathedral. Didn't find anything. Then I moved on."

"Why did you come back?" Daniel asked.

"To check the altars again and wait for the murderer. I hoped he'd pass through, looking where I looked. I wanted to get the clues from him. He knew how to break into museums. I don't know anything about picking locks or disabling security systems. I figured I could trick him into giving up his clues. If that didn't work, I was going to call the police and try and make a deal, I'd give you guys his location in exchange for the clues he'd gathered."

Daniel stared at the community college teacher for a minute. Either this guy was a terrible liar, a master liar, or he was the perfect example of an educated idiot.

Andrew's "plan", if one could call it that, consisted of wandering around all the museums he and Remi had written about, hoping to bump into the killer. Like the killer would be wearing a t-shirt saying, "I'm staking out this museum so I can steal clues to the cryptex." And what would he do if he found him? Convince him to give up the clues he'd been killing for? Riiiight. Oh, but he had a backup plan. Narc on the killer, somehow not get his throat slit, and the cops would reward him with a bunch of stolen artifacts.

A work of criminal genius.

So either Andrew Critchfield was the murderer and had just come up with the Mother of All Bad Alibis, or he was really what he seemed on the surface—a failed academic who still managed to live in an ivory tower and who had just been bitch-slapped by reality.

Or maybe he wasn't what he seemed on the surface. Maybe Andrew was smarter than that. Maybe the dumbass loser image was a smokescreen, hiding a calculating killer. Daniel had seen that before, plenty of times. Serial killers were like molesters, hiding in plain sight, at least as much as they could. Molesters projected an affable, trustworthy image perfected from a lifetime of hiding their true nature. Serial killers also had to hide their true nature, but their impulses, or at least the results of them, proved much harder to hide. You couldn't keep a body quiet like you could a trapped child.

So serial killers tended to be recluses, shunning contact with the outside world, maintaining an image of normality as much as they could.

But they always slipped. Their brutal nature came out, and that made them easy to spot given enough time.

Andrew Critchfield had slipped. Screaming at students. Two fights with strangers.

Was that the extent of his violence? Was he just a frustrated loser living at the margins of society and occasionally lashing out? Or was he more?

The investigation would reveal it all. Baltimore PD was at Critchfield's apartment and office right now conducting a search. They'd take his computers and go through his history and files. It wouldn't be long before they knew a lot more about this guy.

"So when can I go?" Critchfield asked.

"You are under arrest for assaulting Professor Laurent—"

"I didn't assault her!"

Actually, he hadn't but Daniel didn't care. "—for assaulting professor Laurent and for suspicion of three counts of murder."

Critchfield's eyes went wide.

"You think I did it?"

"We'll work all that out eventually. If you're innocent, you have nothing to worry about."

"You idiots!" Critchfield screamed. "You might as well hand that guy the cryptex. Priceless wisdom in the hands of a maniac. Who knows what kind of damage he can do with it! Let me go and get the real killer."

"Tell us more about what you know and that might help us clear this up," Detective Gavers said, keeping his tone reasonable. It was a common tactic to calm down agitated suspects.

This time, it failed.

"Idiots! A bunch of idiots! I almost had the cryptex in my hand and you're handing it off to a killer!"

Critchfield continued, calling the police every name in the book.

Daniel got bored. This wasn't going anywhere, at least not for the moment. He wanted Remi's input. Nodding to Detective Gavers to continue, he stood.

"So tell me your exact route when visiting the museums. Where did you go first?" the detective asked Critchfield as Daniel went out of the interrogation room.

He passed a few feet down the hallway and into the next room. The observation room was dark so the one-way glass would work. Remi stood close to it, staring at Critchfield.

"What do you think?" they asked each other in unison.

Daniel gestured to her. "You first."

The professor glanced at Critchfield again, who could be heard through the microphone demanding to be hired as a special assistant to the police, then back at Daniel.

"I don't know," she said. "I'm not sure he's the killer."

Daniel rolled his eyes and sat in the nearest chair.

"Crap. I'm not sure either."

CHAPTER SEVENTEEN

Sitting in the observation room, Remi couldn't decide who she felt sorrier for, Daniel or herself. She hadn't slept a wink the previous night and it was beginning to wear on her. While she occasionally "pulled an all-nighter," as her students called it, when hot on the trail of some exciting research topic, she wasn't used to all this tension and running around. Poor Daniel, on the other hand, looked wiped out. At least he hadn't seriously injured his elbow when he crashed to the floor with that half-sane man in the interrogation room.

As if reading her thoughts, Daniel absentmindedly rubbed his elbow. He'd been doing that every minute or so ever since the arrest.

She sat down next to him. Critchfield was going through his movements of the past four days. Remi didn't pay any attention. He could very well be lying.

"Tell me why you're not sure it's him," Daniel said.

"Well, he sure is obsessive, and he has motive, it's just physically … " Remi waved her hand in the air, trying to think of the right words.

Daniel fixed her with a look, like she was the one under questioning.

"Physically … what?"

"I can't say for sure. Those security images aren't very good quality, but he just doesn't strike me as the same man."

"He's not as bulky and he moves differently. Critchfield is more energetic but a bit more uncertain in his movements."

"Ah, that's it exactly!"

She would have never been able to put it into words. It seemed that policework was as complex a discipline as medieval studies.

"What else?" Daniel asked.

Remi thought for a minute. Daniel waited. She was beginning to appreciate that methodical side of his nature. It was certainly more worthy of respect than his food choices and general mannerisms.

"I'm not sure he could kill," she said. "He has so much hate inside him, and yet it's an impotent hate. He's never made anything of himself and when he had me alone, the person he might hate more than any other, he didn't try to stab me." Remi hesitated, suddenly unsure of herself. "At least that's my impression. I've never known any criminals, just heard about them. Was a knife found on him or his car?"

"No."

"What do you think? Did he do it?"

Daniel studied the suspect through the one-way glass for a moment. Critchfield was now trying to convince Detective Gavers that only he could lead them to the killer and save the cryptex for humanity, and that Remi was a useless hack who knew nothing about medieval studies. Detective Gavers listened quietly, wearing what Americans called a "poker face."

"I'm on the fence," Daniel said, and didn't look too happy about the admission. "He's obsessive, and he's shown violence and rage in the past, but all those strikes against him being our guy that you just outlined are things I noticed too."

"So you don't think his belief in the cryptex makes him insane?"

"No. It could exist. A respected professor from the Sorbonne believes in it, after all." Daniel gave her a friendly nudge with her elbow.

Remi shifted in her seat, unsure how to take such a relaxed gesture from someone who wasn't a friend. She had a hard time reading Americans. They pretended to be so open and friendly, but that was only on the surface. They could be very difficult to get to know well.

But at least he believed in it. Most of her colleagues, even her boyfriend, thought it was a myth.

"Respected in all my work except with the cryptex," Remi said with a grimace. "Not so respected in that, though."

"Your colleagues don't believe the cryptex exists?"

"No. Too wild an idea."

"Well, I'm not an expert, but lots of weird stuff happened in the Middle Ages. Ever hear about Eilmer of Malmesbury? He was a monk in England who made a set of wings for himself and flew off the abbey tower. They said he made it a furlong. That's like 200 yards."

"It's 220 yards, or 201 meters."

Daniel chuckled. "You're precise. Maybe you should work in a CSI lab."

"No thank you. I'm surprised you've heard of Eilmer of Malmesbury. It's not a very well-known story."

He gave a little shrug, looked away, and didn't answer.

There's something strange about this man, she thought. *He knows far more about history than he lets on, but it slips out sometimes. When it does, he acts embarrassed by it. Hurt, almost.*

I don't think he's very happy at his work.

"Let's watch the interrogation," Remi suggested. "Perhaps the detective will wear him down. Suspects have a hard time keeping up the façade for an extended period."

Daniel half turned in his seat to look at her. "You know, for a university professor you seem to know a lot about how criminals work."

Remi laughed. "Are you suspicious of me now?"

Daniel barked out a laugh. "Teamed up with the actual killer. Wouldn't that be my luck! My new boss would love that. I think she hates me."

"I can sympathize. At the Sorbonne last year, we got a new chair for the history department, more of a political appointee than an actual historian. He started making changes and ignoring the opinions of professors who had been there for decades."

"That's not my situation. The Antiquities Division is new, and I'm even newer."

"So how long have you been in the Antiquities Division?"

"Four days."

Remi looked at him with surprise. He was hunched over, glaring at the suspect through the one-way glass.

"Four days?"

"I got moved from profiling. I was tracking a serial killer, someone who was past due to make a another kill."

"Why did they transfer you from one serial killer to another?"

"I don't know."

Remi suspected he did know. His knowledge of history made him a good fit. So why the reluctance?

If she was going to work effectively with this man, she needed to know more about him. And the best way to do that was offer something of her own.

She paused, uncertain, then dove in.

"I know a bit about the criminal world thanks to my father. He was an officer in the Police Nationale in Paris."

That caught his interest. "Oh yeah? I'd love to meet him sometime. Swap some war stories. I bet he's got a million of them."

"He died some years ago," Remi said, the old loss tugging at her, and the old resentment.

Daniel's face fell. "Oh crap. I'm sorry. Stuck my foot in it again."

"He died very young. Only 53."

In a quieter tone, Daniel asked, "Did he … get killed in the line of duty?"

Remi let out a bitter little laugh. "He would have loved that. No, he did it too himself. Too much work, too much stress, too many cigarettes, too many meals on the go."

Daniel shook his head and grimaced. "Yeah, cigarettes are real bad. I'm so glad I never picked up that habit."

You're missing the point, Hamburger Man.

"I didn't see him much," Remi said.

"Common cop problem," Daniel said, looking back at Critchfield, who was still babbling on about how the world always picked on him. "The thing is that you get so wound up in the work it's easy to lose perspective. You know that if you work a few more hours, you might catch another bad guy, might even save somebody's life. So any day off, or even any day where you only work your allotted shift, makes you feel like you're cheating the public." In a quieter voice he said, "No excuse for skimping on family life, though."

Remi paused, thinking he'd go on. When he didn't, she asked in a happier tone, "So what was your father like? An all-American dad? Lots of baseball games and throwing a football in the park?"

Daniel gave a little shrug. "He would have been. He died when I was five, though."

"Oh, I'm so sorry. Looks like I put my foot on it too."

A ghost of a smile. "The phrase is 'put your foot in it.' But yeah, so it was just me and my mom and our … her boyfriend. She was a history professor at NYU."

"Really?"

"Yeah. European history. She specialized in the Napoleonic era but had a big interest in all periods. She'd spend all day reading two-hundred-year-old letters in some archive in France and then go off to see a Roman villa or Cistercian monastery. People say I'm obsessed with my work. Ha! They should have met her. I never remember her taking a day off. I guess I got it from her."

"So that's why you know so much about history."

"We did a lot of European tours," Daniel said, not looking at her. His face had grown grim. Why? "But I learned on my own too. At Tufts I majored in history with a minor in political science. She loved that. Talked to me endlessly about my coursework."

A weak smile. It didn't last.

"She must be proud of her son catching serial killers," Remi said.

"I wouldn't know," Daniel said curtly. "Speaking of serial killers, if our hunch is correct, the Cryptex Killer is still out there, and we need to find him pronto. Forget this jackass." Daniel made a dismissive wave toward the interrogation room. "We'll keep him in custody just in case, and also to keep him from interfering with the investigation. Don't want him showing up at one of the museums and causing trouble. But we need to work on the assumption that our guy is still out there. So we need to figure out where he's going to strike next. Show me that map again."

Remi pulled out her laptop and they stared at the screen together, showing the map of North America and Europe with points for all the collections that contained medieval items once owned by members of the Cryptex Club.

"Fourteen places," Daniel growled, "Including two in Germany and one in England. Oh, and one in Toronto too. Didn't notice that before. Damn. We'll never get the local police to lock all these down. We can convince some of them, but all of them? No way. We need to narrow this list down. Do you have any ideas?"

Remi stared at the screen. She had been thinking the same thing ever since she had come up with this baffling number of museums and archives. She had studied and studied this map and come up with nothing.

Remi took a deep breath, hoping for a flash of insight. None came.

"I'm stuck," she admitted. "But I think I know someone who might be able to help. Can I get away with making an international phone call on the police station telephone?"

Daniel cracked a grin, his glum mood of a moment before seemingly vanished now that he was back on the hunt again. Remi recognized that look. She'd seen it on her father's face on the rare nights he made it home for dinner after collaring some important criminal.

“Professor, if it helps bag our guy, I can get you anything you want. Let me worry about justifying it to the higher ups. You can call ISIS headquarters for all I care.”

“No one quite so radical,” Remi said with a bemused smile, “Although some would say he’s equally polemic.”

CHAPTER EIGHTEEN

At 87 years of age, Professor Auguste de Villepin's voice may have been gravelly and a bit fainter than it had once been, but it was no less sharp.

"How many times have I told you I'm not going to vote? I don't care what party you're from. Every politician in France is a thief and a liar! I'd guillotine them all given half a chance!"

Remi smiled. "Hello, Professor de Villepin."

Her old advisor recognized her voice instantly. "Remi! How good to hear from you. The department has been much uglier since you left. The younger generation of girls don't make themselves up right. Too tarty. You need to be subtle to grab a man. Have you seen sense and come back to Paris?"

"No, I'm still in America."

"Still casting pearls before swine, eh? Well, just as long as you don't fall in love with one of those Neanderthals."

Remi was glad he couldn't see her blush.

"How are you, professor?" she asked.

"Good. Ignoring the current election by finishing up an article on the church policy of Louis IX. I've found some new documents that will smash Gourcuff's theories to dust. That Breton bastard will never recover. They'll laugh him out of the department in Nantes and he'll be selling newspapers on the street before the next academic term."

"Still fighting all your old rivals, I see."

Remi could hear his smile from across the Atlantic. "Ah, nothing more satisfying, except for a woman."

"So how is Eloise?" That was his second wife, twenty years his junior.

"Oh, fine."

"And Angelique?" That was his current mistress, forty years his junior.

"Splendid. Utterly splendid. What a woman!"

Remi had never asked what they did together. She didn't want to know, and she felt sure Professor de Villepin would tell her given the opportunity.

Before she had a chance to change the subject, her old advisor cut her off.

"You didn't call me in the middle of a weekday just to chitchat. Something's on your mind. Spit it out so I can help."

Remi shook her head. Many graduate students couldn't stand his abrupt ways. She found it endearing. It helped that he was the only professor in the department who had taken her research seriously.

He had also never flirted with her in any serious way. *Don't worry about me,* he would always say. *You're too young. Mature women are better. More experience. Besides, you're in love with the cryptex.*

"I seem to have found myself in a strange place, professor. I'm hunting a serial killer for the FBI. He's after the cryptex."

"You really have landed in the Wild West, haven't you? Go on. Tell me everything. Don't leave out a single detail. It's already evening here, I have a bourbon, and I'm sitting by the fire. My time is yours. Tell me everything."

So she did—laying out the case slowly, methodically, making sure she gave him every detail, no matter how small. She knew she didn't have to explain anything related to the cryptex. Professor de Villepin had read all her papers in draft and given recommendations before their publication. While the cryptex was not his specialty, he had followed Remi's career from the start and was more deeply versed in the era than any living historian.

In the half hour her explanation took, as she sat at a worn old phone at the entrance to the local lockup, at a phone that had been used by countless criminals calling their lawyers or loved ones in desperate hope of freedom, the professor listened in silence, only breaking it two or three times to ask for clarification.

Once she had brought him up to speed, she told him the list of institutions she suspected of having items that might contain the cryptex.

There was a silence over the line. Remi was just about to speak again when Professor de Villepin said abruptly,

"Narrow it down."

"That's what I'm trying to do," she said, impatient.

"Then do it."

"I can't. That's why I called—"

"Yes you can. Narrow it down."

"How?"

"The police might stop him, but this man sounds too clever for your average American policeman. You and your FBI agent need to pick the right spot and be there yourselves. Someone will die tonight if you don't guess right. So narrow it down. You need to think of the most probable. You can't be sure of the right institution, so choose the one that's most probable. Don't just think of the objects themselves, but the people behind the objects, the men and women who bought and preserved them back in the 1930s. It's not the objects you're really chasing, it's the thoughts of those people who formed the Cryptex Club. Get into their heads, the same way your FBI friend gets into the heads of the criminals he pursues."

Remi thought for a minute, and a few institutions became more prominent in her mind than the others.

"The Sanders Collection in Ft. Lauderdale."

"Why?"

"Paul Sanders was prominent in the Cryptex Club. None of his collection has moved since they opened that museum in 1939. Plus, the killer skipped a night. We're assuming that is because he's hurt, but it really might be because he's had to make a long drive."

"Good. Where else?"

"The Museum of Fine Arts in Boston."

"Why?"

"They received the Huxley collection upon his death. Once again, that collection has never been moved. The Cryptex Club often met at Edgar Huxley's mansion in Boston."

"Excellent. Anywhere else?"

"The Ashmolean in Oxford," she said with mounting excitement. "The killer hasn't targeted any institution in Europe. The Cryptex Club would have secreted at least one clue on the other side of the Atlantic as additional security."

"Outstanding, but why not the Alt Glyptothek or Augustiner Museum? Some items ended up at both."

"The war. By the time the Cryptex Club was preparing to hide its clues, Hitler had risen to power and everyone predicted war would break out. While no one could know how the war would go, they didn't want one piece of the puzzle to be on the wrong side of the battle lines."

"So there you have it," Professor de Villepin said triumphantly. "You are as intelligent as you are sensually appealing."

"Flattery will get you nowhere," she said with a grin. "So now we have three places. Which one will he strike next?"

"You tell me."

"I'm … not sure."

"Make an educated guess. If you were the killer, and you most likely have at least two pieces of the puzzle still left to retrieve, what institution would you go for next?"

"I don't know. I'm not a killer."

"You may not have the mind of a killer, but you want the same thing. You are, to be blunt, just as obsessed as he is."

Remi jerked in her chair. The professor's "to be blunt" was a half-apology. From a man who never apologized. Did he think that calling her as obsessed as the murderer would hurt her feelings?

It did, a little.

Because when someone's feelings were hurt, it was usually because a comment came close to the truth.

Or hit it squarely.

"I'm waiting," Professor de Villepin said.

"Not the Ashmolean."

"Why not?"

"Flying to England is a risk. I know the police are searching for me. International flights are monitored, and I might have a criminal record. Also, I wouldn't want to leave the other clues behind. At least one clue, the Gorizia dodecahedron, is a Roman artifact. If airport security realized this, they'd ask if I had permission to transport it."

"So you'd go to the Ashmolean last."

"Yes."

"So of the remaining two institutions, where would you go?"

Remi thought, and did not come up with anything.

She looked at the map on the laptop on her lap.

There must be something I'm missing.

Her gaze flicked over all the points on her map, then hesitated over the High Museum of Art in Atlanta. Hadn't she seen something about that in *Art News* lately?

She went to their website and searched for Ashmolean, finding several hits for one of England's most famous museums. Her old advisor kept quiet, knowing she was deep in thought.

She scrolled down the list of articles until one jumped out at her. Yes, she had seen this a few months ago but had never read it.

The High Museum of Art was hosting an exhibition on ivory artwork called "Ivory Through the Ages: Artworks from Prehistory to the Renaissance." The exhibition had made headlines because animal rights activists had used it as a chance to protest the slaughter of elephants.

Remi clicked on the link to the exhibition, then onto the gallery, scrolling down through the various objects displayed. First came a crude carving of a face from the Paleolithic made from the tusk of a mastodon. Next was a carved reindeer from prehistoric Lapland carved from narwhal tusk. Then came an ivory plaque from Siberia incised with shamanic magical symbols.

Then she came to more familiar territory. A Byzantine ivory diptych, the covers of a psalter or a similar religious book, were delicately carved with an image of the Emperor Alexios III Angelos on one panel, and the scene of the Annunciation on the other. The Virgin Mary's upturned face as the angel came down from Heaven to tell her she would be the Mother of God showed a serenity and tenderness that had been preserved for eight hundred years.

Focus.

She kept scrolling.

And then she hit it.

A fourteenth century ivory pyxis, a cylindrical box priests used to carry the consecrated host. The caption to the photo said it was on loan from the Ashmolean Museum.

Remi's limbs trembled so much her laptop fell off her lap and she had to grab it before it crashed to the concrete floor.

She must have cried out, because her old professor broke his silence.

"You alright?"

"Yes," she gasped, cleared her throat, steadied her laptop, and went on. "Yes. I found it. The killer doesn't need to go to the Ashmolean. I think the artifact where the cryptex is hidden is in the United States, on loan to the High Museum of Art in Atlanta."

"You said cryptex and not a clue to the cryptex. Why?"

As usual Professor de Villepin's direct manner cut through her confused thoughts, forcing her to get them in order before his direct question was followed up by an even more direct criticism. When she had been in graduate school, he had reminded her of a more educated version of a Marine drill sergeant.

"Because the cryptex itself would be the best candidate to send overseas," she said. "You would want to keep that the safest," she said, her thoughts coalescing as the words came out of her mouth. "Also the artifact it's in. It's a pyxis, used to contain the Eucharist. The flesh of Christ. That makes it the holiest object in the church besides the chalice containing the blood of Christ, the communion chalice, and I don't see how you could hide the cryptex in a chalice."

"How can you hide the cryptex in a pyxis?" her professor was asking now, not leading.

"I … don't know. A false bottom perhaps. The lid looks thick and oversized too. Perhaps it's in there. In all the mentions of the cryptex, no one actually gives its dimensions. So we have no real idea how big it is. I've always thought it wasn't all that big."

"Why not? You haven't mentioned this theory in any of your papers."

"Because I have no evidence. But it comes from the measurements of the Roman dodecahedron from Gorizia. It was only discovered in the nineteenth century. Later sources say it's a clue to unlocking the cryptex. How could that be when the cryptex was made centuries before its discovery? I think the key lies in its shape. Each of its twelve faces is a pentagon, so five edges to each face. Also, each face has a much smaller hole in the center."

She paused, looked around to make sure no one was within easy listening distance, and continued in a whisper.

"I think the Cryptex Club found that with so many dimensions on the surface of the dodecahedron, they could align various faces or holes to match the distance from one edge of the cryptex to its various squares. A bit like the scale on a map. That gave the sequence of the numbers or letters on the cryptex you have to turn to unlock it. I think the clues actually don't provide the location to the cryptex, since the members of the Cryptex Club would already know that, but to the combination to unlock it. That would be difficult to remember, and dangerous to write down in multiple places, so they set down the combination in various clues and scattered them across Europe and North America."

"Wait a moment. So you're saying they opened the cryptex?"

Remi took in a deep breath and let it out slowly. "Yes."

"So why no big revelation?"

"That I don't know, and there's no point in theorizing. Maybe there's a puzzle within a puzzle they couldn't solve. Maybe … there's nothing. That's hard to face but I have to accept that as a possibility. And in any case, the idea that they managed to unlock the cryptex is really just a hunch. It doesn't even qualify as a theory."

"If I've learned anything from watching your career, Remi, it's that when you get a hunch in your pretty little head, it always ends up being true."

It didn't at that museum in Washington, D.C.

"Hopefully we'll get to test that," Remi said.

"And you didn't share this hunch with that FBI agent, whatshisname?"

"Daniel."

"Does this Daniel have a last name?"

"Walker," Remi corrected. "Agent Walker."

"You're withholding information from the FBI because you want a chance to open the cryptex yourself."

Remi bowed her head, muttering a "yes" like an abashed child.

Even if she didn't have the phone pressed to her ear, even if she had hung up a moment before, she could have probably heard Professor de Villepin's laughter reaching over the Atlantic and bursting through the concrete walls of the police station.

"Perfect! Absolutely perfect! You're getting the Americans to do your legwork and you get the prize. That's the best thing I've heard in years! Good for you. Make those Neanderthals muck about with the police work while you make the biggest historical discovery of your generation. Well done."

"D—Agent Walker is not a Neanderthal," Rem said, slightly irritated, while also amused by how approving her former advisor was of her scheme.

"Of course not. He has a PhD from the Sorbonne and his paper on Carolingian trade routes got a standing ovation at the Medievalist Institute last summer. Oh, all right. I'm being uncharitable. He's probably decent enough as a policeman. And he'll be toting a gun like all Americans. Make sure he uses it. And I'm serious about that, Remi. You are playing a very dangerous game. That killer sounds like a religious maniac, like the Islamists we have filling up the *banlieues*. They cut off another head last week. Make sure the next one isn't your own."

"I'll be careful," Remi promised. The image of that poor security guard rose up in her mind's eye, turning her stomach.

"And be careful of your Agent Daniel. Withholding information from a police investigation is illegal in France, if I recall, and probably is illegal even in the Wild West. If he finds out you've been holding out on him, the next person he investigates might be you."

CHAPTER NINETEEN

While waiting for Remi to finish her phone call, Daniel sat in the observation room watching Detective Gavers interrogate Critchfield. The longer the interrogation went on, the more Daniel felt his and Remi's hunch was correct. Critchfield wasn't a killer. Daniel doubted if he even had the intelligence to figure out where the clues were hidden.

He'd seen plenty of people like this in college, insecure people who thought reading a lot of obscure books made them intelligent, who thought a piece of paper from an institution of higher learning was a worthy substitute for character. Who thought they were better than everyone else, but secretly knew they weren't.

They didn't become killers. They didn't have the strength.

Real scholars like Remi were one in a hundred in that crowd. Besides a couple of professors, he didn't meet a single true intellectual during his undergraduate coursework. It was one of the things that made him not pursue history and get his doctorate.

That and how his mother reacted when he had finally summoned the courage to tell her what happened between him and Uncle Ray.

She had broken up with him a few years before, shortly after Daniel's fifteenth birthday when Daniel had had enough. Uncle Ray had taken him on one of his regular drives, stopping at an isolated spot. Daniel, now five-ten and a fullback on the high school football team, slugged him. Ray gave him such a look of shock that Daniel apologized.

Decades later, he still hated himself for apologizing. Still hated himself for that weakness. For thinking that all the attention Ray had given him, all the gifts, all the kindness, had been anything more than a tool to get what he wanted.

Daniel had run off, hitching his way home.

Ray had only seen Mom a few times after that, and always made sure to see her alone. Then, maybe a month later, she came home in tears.

"I don't know why he wants to break it off," she sobbed.

Daniel knew.

But he didn't have the strength to tell her why.

It was only when he was almost twenty-one that he found the courage to do so. Even then he had to do it on a long-distance call.

"How could you say something like that about a man who showed you nothing but kindness? All those times he took you to ball games, all those birthday and Christmas presents … he spent more time with you than with me!"

"Mom, why would I make this up?"

"I don't know. You act crazy sometimes. You were always withdrawn and sullen around me. You gave me so much trouble growing up. It was because you lost your father. Well, Ray tried to be that for you."

"No he didn't, he—"

"He was so kind to you, and then you stab him in the back. Really, Daniel, I don't know what's wrong with you."

And then she hung up. And Daniel's family life, such as it was, ended.

He spent more time with you than with me.

Daniel had never asked her what she meant by that, because even now he didn't want to know. Had she suspected the truth all this time? Had she turned a blind eye because she didn't want to lose a man she loved, like she had lost Dad?

The door to the observation room opened. Daniel jerked and almost fell out of his seat.

Remi stood there, outlined in the brighter light of the hallway.

"I know where he's going to strike next," she said.

"Do you?" She'd been wrong before. Still, Daniel put too much heat in that question, his earlier thoughts soaking into the new conversation.

I'm sick of having my childhood affect my adulthood.

"Yes, I'm as sure of it as I can be." She closed the door and sat down beside him. Neither bothered to look at the continuing interrogation.

"Your professor give you some new information?"

"No, he helped me figure it out for myself. He's good at that. Remember I told you they hid one clue in the Ashmolean in Oxford? I discovered a medieval church relic from that museum is on loan to the High Museum of Art in Atlanta."

Daniel sat up straighter. "Oh. And this is public knowledge?"

"The piece is photographed on the exhibition website."

Daniel thought for a moment, his thumb tapping against his thigh. "He would have seen that. I bet he trolls through the Internet constantly. He probably read every one of Andrew Critchfield's articles and laughed his ass off. He wouldn't be laughing about this temporary exhibition, though."

"We need to go there."

"All right. I got the local P.D. to alert all the museums. Told them to lock down. Got some pushback from some of them, including the High Museum. Doesn't matter. We'll go there and strongarm them into cooperating. Flashing a badge and hinting a threat works wonders with spineless academics. No offense. We'll lay a trap for him."

Remi raised an eyebrow. "We?"

"Yes. We." Daniel raised a warning finger. "As long as you behave. No running after serial killers, all right?"

"All right."

She agreed way too quickly.

Daniel leaned forward a little, watching her reaction.

"Remember what happened to poor Ted Peterson?"

The corner of Remi's mouth twitched. Her eyes unfocused for a second, and Daniel knew she was seeing that photo again. If the room had been brighter, Daniel guessed he'd have seen her go pale.

"I remember," she said in a soft voice. "I won't go running after anyone."

Daniel studied her for a moment longer. She gave a little nod, looked him in the eye, and nodded again.

"I won't," she said.

I hope that's true, Daniel thought.

* * *

They arrived at the High Museum at nine o'clock, well after it had already closed. Like in Hartford, a car from the local police department had picked them up and drove them straight there. Unlike in Hartford, the Atlanta PD had been smart enough to send an unmarked car with an officer in civilian clothes. He was a big, long-limbed man with deep frown lines and a buzz cut. While Daniel could have spotted him as a cop from a mile off, he did look like he could handle himself.

Good. They might just need some extra muscle tonight.

Remi had slept the entire flight, wiped out from all the stress and her lack of sleep the previous night. Daniel had slept too, knowing he'd need the energy. Both had grabbed large coffees as soon as they got out of the terminal.

Now they were geared up and ready to go.

The museum was a modern white concrete building with lots of windows and walkways set on a hill in the center of downtown. It looked more like the home of a tech company than a collection of art. To one side stood an older brick church, but the rest of the nearby buildings were modern, collections of offices or apartments. A four-lane road ran along the front, and not far in the distance loomed the skyscrapers of the city's business district.

The killer had a very public place to break into this time. The open spaces, the busy streets full of traffic and pedestrians, acted as a shield to any intruders.

The officer drove the unmarked car around back to show them the layout. After passing the church and turning left to get to the rear of the museum, Daniel saw the chink in the High Museum's armor. The street running behind the museum was only two lanes and poorly lit, more of an access road than a place for regular traffic. Even though it was only 9:00 PM, theirs was the only car. Opposite the museum was a strip of grass and a screen of trees. Only a few city lights shone through the foliage.

"What's beyond those trees?" Daniel asked.

"A metro station. A pedestrian underpass leads to the museum. There's a hot dog vendor at the museum end of the underpass who's a police informant. Usually calls in drug dealers but we got him on duty for this right now."

"That's great, thanks."

"Wish we knew more about what the perp looks like."

While it wasn't meant as a criticism, Daniel felt stung. After three murders, they still didn't have any physical description except for what they got off the poor-quality surveillance cameras.

"The underpass will feel like a trap to him," Daniel said. "He'll come through those trees."

"He'd make quite a show for the station security cameras sneaking around back, cutting through the trees, and hopping the fence. We've warned the station security."

Daniel nodded. The Atlanta police were on the ball. Except …

"Are the station security guards armed?" Daniel asked.

"No."

"Is the hot dog vendor armed?"

"You kidding?"

Daniel let out a weary sigh. Remi gave him a sympathetic look.

"Tell them not to engage with any suspicious characters. This guy is armed and extremely dangerous."

"Already have."

"Good. How many officers are we getting?"

"Just me and my partner. He's already at the museum. And we're right in downtown. A patrol car is always less than five minutes' response time away."

"All right," Daniel said. He would have preferred more, but with Atlanta's high crime rate, getting two plainclothesmen and a civilian informant was actually pretty generous.

As if sensing Daniel's disappointment, the police officer added, "The security guards in the museum are armed."

That didn't help Mortimer Phelps.

They looped around to the other side of the museum, a four-lane road called 15th Street, and found this quiet as well. Here the museum fronted only office buildings, which had rapidly emptied out on the warm, clear spring evening. Only a few lights burned in the windows, a few workaholic diehards who had managed to resist the temptation of a fine evening.

"This looks like a better place to come at the museum," Daniel said.

"I was thinking the same thing," the cop agreed. "But we'll see him coming thanks to the cameras. He may be good at getting through security systems, but it will still take time. We'll be able to get to the location he's breaking in and bust him."

"I hope so," Remi said in a soft voice from the back seat.

Daniel turned and gave her a reassuring smile.

Or at least tried to. Hard to be convincing when you're not convinced yourself.

"Nervous?" he asked.

"Of course. Are you?"

Daniel looked her in the eye. "Being overconfident when trying to collar a suspect is a good way to get hurt. I'm nervous in every situation like this. Excited too. I like the hunt. Just like you with your medieval mysteries."

Remi cracked a smile. So did Daniel, a genuine one this time.

The unmarked car pulled into an underground parking garage. A security guard manned a little booth at the entrance. He came out to greet him.

"No vehicles have come in or out except museum staff I recognize," he said, answering Daniel's question before he had a chance to ask it.

"Anyone else due to come in?" Daniel asked.

"No, sir," the security guard said.

"Good. Lock this parking lot up tight, and double check every entrance. Officer, let's park and get to work," Daniel said, dispensing with the introductions.

They needed to get into position fast. While they had taken the earliest plane they could to Atlanta, they had arrived far too late in the evening for Daniel's liking. He worried he wouldn't have time to check out the extensive building and set up before the killer made an appearance.

Assuming he did. Remi had been wrong twice already, first with the museum in D.C., and again with the cathedral in Hartford. While she was a valuable asset for the case, she didn't understand killers or police procedure. She jumped to conclusions too quickly, didn't think them through.

Of course, she didn't have the training for that, despite having a cop for a dad, and she didn't have time to learn.

The lack of time was the real problem for both of them. Daniel had never dealt with a serial killer who moved this rapidly. It flew in the face of all received wisdom about their kind and made it ten times harder to predict what he'd do next.

He could have predicted what Remi did next, though. She was already running up the steps to the museums like some schoolgirl who had heard her favorite boy band was inside.

"Wait up, Remi!" Daniel said, huffing up the stairs after her.

"I need to see it!" she called back without turning around or slowing.

"We need to catch a criminal," Daniel said.

Priorities, professor. Priorities.

CHAPTER TWENTY

Remi gazed at the ivory pyxis, feeling something akin to awe. Could this really contain the cryptex?

She stood in the temporary exhibition space of the High Museum, up on the first floor just above the entrance hall. Around her were some of the greatest works of art ever made in ivory. To her right was the tiny Venus of Brassempouy, only the size of her thumb and which at 23,000 years old was one of the oldest representations of a human face. To her left was an entire elephant tusk from 19th century Congo with hunting and trading scenes carved in bas-relief. Beyond were displayed more treasures from all parts of the globe and all periods of history.

But Remi had eyes for only one display case.

The pyxis was large for its kind of object, about as big around as a dessert plate, and as tall as a pint glass. It had obviously come from a male elephant, which have thicker tusks than females, and cut right from the base of the tusk.

The outside was carved with the image of a man in the costume of English nobility. Remarkable. The ivory had made from sub-Saharan Africa all the way up to England at a time when it most of the ivory trade was being siphoned off by the Almohad and Abbasid Caliphates. The Europeans had searched elsewhere for ivory in that era, trading northern peoples for narwhal tusks from Lapland and as far away as Greenland.

But narwhal tusks aren't nearly as large, and some long-forgotten English artisan had wanted to fashion a pyxis out of a single piece of ivory. So he had somehow gotten his hands on a rare elephant tusk, making the object even more valuable.

The perfect place to hide a one-of-a-kind artifact.

Was it really inside? Remi had to resist the urge to grab the fire extinguisher hanging from a nearby wall and smashing the display case to find out. While the pyxis had its lid on, Remi judged that most of the interior space would be hollow to hold the Communion wafers. So that left either a false bottom or a hollow lid.

It wouldn't take long to find out. Just five minutes would probably be enough.

"Come on. We need to get into position."

Daniel's voice took her out of her daydream. She took one last look at the pyxis and followed him, her heart filled with longing.

* * *

The Chosen One was ready, and yet still he doubted. The warm Atlanta night had grown quiet in this part of downtown, where office buildings had closed and few people were about. Further away, he could hear traffic and sinful music, but here was a good place to watch, and wait.

He now had all the clues he needed to unlock the cryptex. The previous night he had broken into the Strayer Military History Museum in Fayetteville, North Carolina.

It had been surprisingly easy. The museum was closed for major renovations, the interior clogged with scaffolding and dust. At first, as he crept through galleries of shrouded display cases and cleared out dioramas, he feared the exhibit might have been moved, but God answered his prayers and the golden halberd held by one of the bodyguards of King Sigismund of Luxembourg remained in its place in the medieval arms and armor gallery. Even better, it wasn't behind glass, instead making up part of a display of mannequins dressed in armor in the center of the room.

The Chosen One had wrenched the blade off the end of the wooden shaft, retrieved a piece of parchment hidden inside, and replaced the blade on the end of the shaft as best he could. It wouldn't pass close inspection, but God willing no one would notice the blade being a bit off kilter, the end of the wooden shaft a bit abraded, amid all those swords and spears and lances.

Even if a museum worker did notice the damage, they would probably blame the construction crew.

He had broken the halberd as quietly as he could. With the museum closed and much of the collection in storage, the Strayer Museum had only posted one security guard. The Chosen One had decided not to sacrifice him. Instead, he slipped out of the museum, the last piece of the puzzle in hand, restarted the burglar alarm and security cameras, and locked the door he had used to enter.

Now he stood in a quiet Atlanta business block, waiting to make the final step. As far as he knew, no one in Fayetteville had noticed the break-in. That put him yet another step ahead of the police.

But to not make the sacrifice … that felt wrong. That was going against God's plan. To take one of God's gifts without giving back in the form of a sacrifice was selfish, a sin. The Chosen One hoped that He, in His Divine Mercy, would allow him this favor for the sake of his quest.

"I will sacrifice two in this place," the Chosen One whispered.

The clock on a nearby bank building said 11:30 PM. Almost time. The streets would get no emptier until the bars closed at 2:30 AM. That was too long to wait. While he was dressed in a convincing disguise that would stave off any uncomfortable questions, loitering here any longer only increased the risk of arousing suspicion. Even dressed as he was, a lone man loitering on an abandoned street always attracted attention.

It was time to move in. It was time to finish this.

CHAPTER TWENTY ONE

Daniel sprinted down the darkened museum corridor, huffing and puffing and cursing the Hawaiian pizza he had eaten with the security guards for dinner. Beside him ran Officer Rogers, one of the plainclothes cops. The crackle on his walkie talkie told him one of the security guards was on his way.

All three were converging on a door on 15th St. next to the entrance to the underground parking lot. A security guard posted in the camera room had spotted someone picking the lock on that door.

Another crackling voice came on the walkie talkie Officer Rogers carried. It was from his partner posted on the far end of the museum. He was running for the location too, but it was clear he would not make it in time.

It was up to Daniel and Rogers.

And that security guard, whatever his name was, who only carried a nightstick and a can of pepper spray.

Better not let him get there first, Daniel thought. *Our perp has a taste for security guards.*

He picked up speed, a stitch in his side making it feel like someone was jabbing a knitting needle deep into his flesh. Daniel ignored it and kept running.

They passed through a gallery of nineteenth century American landscapes, onto a landing half blocked by some ugly modern sculpture, and down a set of stairs.

Daniel and Officer Rogers stopped.

"Was it down that hallway or through the Chinese gallery?" Daniel gasped.

"Uh … damn." Officer Rogers got on the radio and asked the security guard in the camera room the same question. Daniel cursed himself for not studying the floor plan better. But they had only arrived a few hours before, and this place was a giant maze. Why did modern architecture have to be so damn complicated? Just lay the damn museum out so you can find everything!

The guard at the camera room came back with a quick reply. "Through the first Chinese gallery, take a left into the jade room and you'll see a door marked 'staff only.' Go through that and you'll be in a storage room. The outside door leads into that."

Daniel grabbed the walkie talkie from Rogers and, as they ran into the Chinese gallery, spoke into it.

"The security guard who's running for the location, whatever your name is—"

"Bob," Officer Rogers said, running beside him.

"Bob. Do not approach the intruder. I repeat, do not approach the intruder."

Bob's voice came through the radio.

"I'm already there. Hey!" There was clatter as if the radio fell. Faintly they could hear the sound of a scuffle.

Daniel and the plainclothes officer drew their guns. They passed through a long gallery full of Chinese porcelain and took a left into a small room filled with jade artworks.

Daniel wrenched open a door with a sign saying "Staff Only" and rushed into a dimly lit storage room, Officer Rogers right behind him.

And then they stopped.

The place was huge, running half the length of the building. Long metal shelves reaching almost up to the high ceiling that lined both walls. The shelving units ran about fifteen feet in length, with blind spots in between. Partially blocking the passageway running along the center of the storage room stood statues, empty display cases, even a broken drinking fountain.

Daniel saw a million places to hide.

The walkie talkie in Daniel's hand crackled to life.

"Are you in the storage area?" the guard at the camera room asked. "I can't see you. There aren't any cameras in that area."

Of course, there isn't. Why would there be? But thanks for giving away our position.

Daniel turned off the walkie talkie in disgust and clipped it on his belt.

Silence.

Which way was that entrance door? Trying to remember the blueprint of the building he had studied for all too short a time, Daniel thought it was to the left, but he couldn't be sure.

The sound of a soft step in that direction made him sure.

Daniel and Rogers exchanged glances and crept a little forward to a space between two units of the metal shelving. Where there was a gap between shelves, Daniel ducked behind the next shelf and Rogers darted across the open space in the middle of the room to hide behind the shelf on the opposite wall.

There they paused, waiting for the intruder to make a move.

For a long, excruciating moment he didn't; then came the soft scrape of a shoe on the concrete floor.

It sounded like it was on the opposite end of the shelf behind which Daniel hid.

Making eye contact with Officer Rogers, he signaled that the cop should cover him while he himself went ahead.

Steeling his resolve and reminding himself that he had a gun while the killer hopefully only carried a knife, Daniel stepped out of the cover and crept forward. His footsteps sounded like an elephant's.

He reminded himself that was only his fears acting up in his mind.

Focusing down the barrel of his 9mm, he tried to remain calm. He was ten feet away from the end of the shelving now. Eight. Five. Was that nervous breathing he could hear?

Daniel stopped. Took two steps to the right to put some distance between himself and the corner of the shelving. The shelf was open metalwork, but as luck would have it the entire unit was filled with wooden boxes so he couldn't see a thing of the man he now felt sure stood beyond it.

Daniel paused for a second. Given the silence from around that corner of shelving, the killer had almost certainly heard him.

Steeling himself for the violence to come, Daniel advanced, moving to the right to put more room between him and the corner, hoping to allow a precious extra half second before the Cryptex Killer could reach him.

A shadow stepped out from the dim area behind the shelf, raising one hand.

"Freeze!" Daniel and the stranger shouted at the same time. Daniel started to squeeze the trigger …

… then stopped as he recognized the security guard.

The guard let out a deep breath of relief, lowering his pepper spray.

"I almost maced you," he said.

"I almost shot you," Daniel replied.

The security guard's eyes bugged.

"I thought he got you," Daniel said. "What was that sound on the radio?"

"Bumped into a mannequin. Scared the crap outta me."

Daniel rolled his eyes. Amateurs. He was surrounded by amateurs.

The rapid sound of receding footsteps made them both turn. A dark shape ducked behind a statue.

"You! Stay where you are!"

Daniel sprinted along the passageway as the shape flitted between two shelves. All Daniel got a chance to see was a man dressed all in black.

Easy now. Don't let him get a jump on you.

Daniel whipped around the corner of the shelving, once again leaving plenty of space so he couldn't get slashed with that knife.

He was just in time to see a staff door slam shut.

"Damn it! He's in the museum."

He heard the security guard give a warning message on his walkie talkie. Daniel and Officer Rogers came to the door and hesitated. They glanced at each other and Daniel could tell they were thinking the same thing: what if it was a trap?

Daniel nodded to the officer, who, gripping his gun, yanked open the door with his free hand. Daniel found himself aiming at nothing but an empty doorway.

Hurried footsteps receded to the right.

Cursing, Daniel rushed through, the police officer and security guard close at his heels. All Daniel could see was darkened exhibit halls.

"We're going to lose him!" Daniel said.

The security guard got on his walkie talkie again. "Frank, you still in the camera room?"

"Yeah," Frank's voice crackled out of the cheap radio. "I just saw the intruder head into the African gallery. I think he's going to take the east stairs up."

"Is there a shortcut?" Daniel asked, already huffing and puffing.

"No," the security guard said.

"Tell the other officer to go to the ivory exhibition," Daniel said.

As the security guard did so, they passed through a long pair of galleries filled with African sculptures.

"He's climbing the steps!" Frank called through the radio.

Briefly Daniel thought that if the previous museums had assigned enough security guards to the night shift so that one could always stay in the camera room while the others went on rounds, there might never have been any murders. It was only the police presence here that allowed Frank to sit watching cameras all night.

Daniel took the stairs two at a time, feeling like his heart was about to tear apart like tissue paper. He really needed to get in better shape.

They came to a foyer. Statues in niches along the walls looked down at them. Four hallways branched off from it.

The security guard got on his walkie talkie. "Hey Frank, talk to us!"

"He's in the ivory exhibition. Oh crap, so's the professor!"

* * *

Remi knelt, pepper spray in hand, behind the display case housing the pyxis. Distant shouts and the sound of running feet drawing closer echoed through the darkened exhibition rooms. Only the dim red lights over the emergency exits were lit, and they cast the room in an eerie glow as if of a distant vision of hell.

Remi couldn't believe she had ducked out of the camera room and bolted down here. Instinct told her the killer would give Daniel and the others the slip and come up here. It was all on camera and the security guard at the cameras would be sure to tell the police where to follow him—and from what she heard they were—but he'd make it here first. He'd get a few precious moments alone with the pyxis.

Perhaps enough to snatch it and make his getaway.

She couldn't let that happen.

With an almost maternal feeling of duty, she knew she had to protect the pyxis and the secrets it contained.

The sound of running feet grew louder, closer, then suddenly stopped.

Remi tensed. Heavy breathing came from the entrance to the exhibition.

Then the running started again, straight for her hiding place.

Without consciously doing so, Remi leapt up, holding the pepper spray in one hand and flicking on a flashlight in the other.

"Stop!" she shouted.

A burly, middle-aged man in black slacks, matching shirt, and priest's collar jerked back. For a second, he froze in shock. Remi flicked on the flashlight and shone it in his face.

"Stay where you are!" she ordered, surprised at how strong her voice came out.

To her surprise, he did.

Her next surprise came when he started shouting at her in Italian.

Remi spoke Italian fairly well but being faced with a killer screaming imperiously at her in a darkened exhibition hall killed her language ability. She felt like a B student surprised with the hardest pop quiz ever.

The killer gestured at the pyxis and shouted something that included the words "Pope" and "woman."

"Pope" was said with considerably more respect than "woman."

He took a step forward, his frowning face looking demonic in the wavering glow of her flashlight.

Another flashlight shone on them.

"Freeze!" Daniel's voice shouted. "Hands in the air!"

The man put his hands higher but otherwise didn't move.

"On your knees! NOW!"

He shouted something in Italian. Remi, thinking fast, managed to say in passable Italian.

"You are under arrest. He will shoot you if you don't get on the floor."

Grumbling, scowling, the killer got to his knees and then lay on the floor, putting his hands behind his head with his fingers interlaced.

It looks like he used to the procedure, Remi observed.

The man shook like a leaf but still didn't do as he was told.

Daniel huffed over, still out of breath from his chase through the museum, put a knee on the intruder's back, and cuffed him.

"What did I tell you about chasing serial killers through museums?" he snapped at Remi as he hauled the intruder to his feet.

Remi smiled. "I saw you three on the cameras. You were never going to catch him yourselves."

"What's that supposed to mean?"

"I think you need to take up jogging. Or tennis. It's good exercise."

"I'm too busy catching bad guys," Daniel said, giving the prisoner a shake.

"Then you should definitely take up jogging," Remi said.

“Everyone’s a comedian,” Daniel grumbled. “Let’s get this guy down to the station and get to the bottom of this.”

CHAPTER TWENTY TWO

For the third time in as many days, Daniel found himself in a police interrogation room with someone he had arrested as the Cryptex Killer.

It was the familiar scene—concrete box of a room, one way glass along one wall, bad coffee on the table, and a suspect handcuffed to an uncomfortable plastic chair.

The suspect, however, was different. Very different.

He was a well-kept man of about fifty, with a neatly trimmed black beard, the olive skin and brown eyes of someone from the Mediterranean, wearing black slacks and shirt with a priest's collar.

Plus he was speaking urgently in Italian. Not babbling nervously like George Hansen, not ranting and raving like Andrew Critchfield, by desperately trying to make himself understood as if he had great news to share.

He was also issuing orders left, right, and center.

Orders sounded the same in any language. This guy didn't seem to appreciate the fact that he was under arrest. Typical narcissist. Thought he was in charge of any situation. The annals of serial killers were full of his type.

At least that was as much as Daniel could make out from his university knowledge of Latin and a bit of French he remembered from his travels. Not a sound enough linguistic basis from which to interrogate a suspect.

Remi spoke Italian, because of course she did, but she was acting far too eager to be allowed to talk with this guy. Daniel had banished her to the observation room with strict instructions not to interfere. He couldn't afford to have her prejudice a suspect.

Daniel was confused. After some initial hesitation, the guy hadn't resisted arrest and had no weapon on him. Plus, Remi had told him he was pleading innocence.

But if he wasn't the killer, then what was he? Was he really a priest? And if he was, why would a priest know how to pick locks and use that skill to break into a museum?

This guy was the criminal type for sure, which made his priest's collar a disguise. And someone wearing a disguise and breaking into the museum had to be the Cryptex Killer.

Right?

A uniformed officer poked his head into the interrogation room.

"We've found a temporary translator who speaks Italian until we can get an official one."

Daniel and Officer Rogers turned to him.

"Who did you get?" Daniel asked.

"Luigi. Runs Pizza Paradiso. A favorite of the precinct."

Daniel blinked. "You brought me a pizza guy?"

The officer shrugged. "We don't know anyone else who speaks Italian. We had him sign a nondisclosure agreement. Everything's above board."

"Did he bring any pizza with him?" Daniel asked.

"No," the officer replied, puzzled.

"Then send him away."

The officer gaped. "Really?"

"No, not really. Get him in here!"

"Uh, OK."

The officer ducked back out of the interrogation room and returned a minute later with a short Italian man with an ample belly, still wearing a stained apron. The smell of pizza radiated from him, making Daniel's stomach rumble. That chase through the museum had left him hungry.

"You must be Luigi," Daniel said.

"Yes, I am. You want me to translate for you?" the pizza man replied with just a trace of an Italian accent.

"You from Italy?"

"I was born in Palermo but moved to the United States when I was a teenager. We always spoke Italian at home."

"Good enough. I want you to ask this guy why he broke into the High Museum."

Luigi goggled at him. "A priest broke into the art museum?"

"Yes. Well, we don't know if he's really a priest. Why don't you ask him that too?"

"Shall I read him his rights? If you give them to me, I can translate them."

"This isn't a television show. Ask him what I said to ask him!" Daniel growled.

This priestly burglar did not have the right to remain silent and he did not have the right to an attorney. If he was guilty, this case had drawn on long enough and Daniel wanted it ended. If he was innocent, they needed to find that out right now so they could figure out the Cryptex Killer's next step.

Luigi knelt in front of the suspect, who put his hand on the pizza man's head. Daniel resisted the urge to roll his eyes.

The two spoke for a few minutes in Italian, Luigi acting more and more astounded, politely interrupting the suspect several times to ask questions.

Finally, Daniel lost patience.

"Hey, pizza man, care to share with the rest of the class?"

Luigi said something kindly to the suspect, then got to his feet.

"He says he is a monk from the Monastery of St. Adrian of Nicomedia near Ravenna. That's in northern Italy."

"I know where it is," Daniel said, impatient. "If he's a monk, why is he dressed like a priest?"

"A monk can also be a priest," Luigi explained. "They are called religious priests. The priests attached to churches that you are more familiar with are diocesan priests."

"Oh. Is St. Adrian of Nicomedia the patron saint of burglars or something?"

"No, he's the patron saint of guards," Luigi said, growing irritated. Daniel didn't care. He didn't exactly have a lot of good memories involving churches.

"So why was this guy breaking into the museum?"

"He says his order heard about the murders in the museums and sent him to save something called a cryptex from being stolen."

Daniel blinked, looked at the priest, and looked back at the pizza man.

"You ever heard of the cryptex before?" Daniel asked.

Luigi shook his head. "No, what is it?"

Daniel decided to play dumb. You often found out more that way.

"No idea. Ask him what the thing is and why he thought he was better off stealing it than the other guy breaking into museums."

Although the one-way glass separating the interrogation room from the observation room was soundproof, Daniel imagined he could hear

Remi's squeal of frustration. This was another reason he didn't want her here. She was too obsessed and would have been babbling with this so-called monk about the cryptex, telling him everything she knew and not getting any information in return.

Luigi and the monk/priest spoke for another minute.

"He says the cryptex is a medieval object that contains some sort of secret. His order is entrusted to guard that secret. This is why they honor St. Adrian of Nicomedia. When they heard of the murders, they knew someone had learned of its location and so his abbot sent him to stop the cryptex from being stolen."

Daniel cocked his head and studied the prisoner. "Why him? Because he knows how to pick locks?"

Luigi looked embarrassed. "Before receiving the grace of God he was a burglar."

"Wonderful," Daniel grunted. "So what's this secret the cryptex holds?"

Luigi turned and asked the prisoner, who gave a short answer. Luigi looked surprised, asked something else, and got what sounded like a no.

"Well?" Daniel asked. He hated being left out of conversations like this. It would have been ten times worse with Remi, because she would have been so eager that she would have forgotten to translate for him.

"He says he doesn't know what the secret is."

"Seriously? They're have a whole monastery set up in Italy for this thing and they don't even know what the secret is? I'm supposed to believe that?"

Luigi looked offended. "A priest wouldn't lie."

"Don't assume he's a priest."

"It's morning in Italy by now, we can call the monastery," the pizza man said.

"Good idea. Ask him for the number."

Luigi spoke with the prisoner again, then turned back to him.

"It's a very remote monastery and they don't have a phone."

"Everyone has a phone."

"He says they try to isolate themselves from the world as much as possible. Therefore, they don't have any phones. No internet either."

Daniel couldn't decide who he wanted to slap more, the prisoner for lying to him or Luigi for being so gullible.

“Then answer me this, Sherlock, if they don’t have any phones or internet, how did they hear about a string of robberies that only started happening a few days ago?”

Luigi blinked, thought for a moment, and spoke to the prisoner in Italian.

“He says they have agents in Ravenna who scour the news and academic articles for information about the cryptex.”

“How convenient. Fine. Give me the contact info for one of these ‘agents in Ravenna.’”

“He says only the abbot has that information.”

Daniel hissed through his teeth in frustration. The worst part about being a cop had to be that everyone lied to you. No, the worst part about being a cop was that you weren’t allowed to beat people over the head with a large, heavy object for lying to you.

The prisoner said something, and he and the pizza man started talking again. Daniel jumped a little when he heard the supposed monk say “Remi Laurent.”

Luigi turned back to Daniel. “He says there’s a university professor named Remi Laurent who he wants to speak with. He says you should get into contact with her too. She’s the only one who can find the killer.”

Daniel thought he heard another shout from the observation room. While he knew that was impossible through the soundproof glass, it didn’t matter. He’d bet a thousand dollars Remi had shouted.

He had better go talk with her before she burst in here.

“Get more information about him. I want to know when he got here, if he went anywhere else first, anything you can get. And ask him again what’s inside the cryptex.”

Luigi nodded. “I’ll try.”

Leaving Luigi and the prisoner in the care of an officer, Daniel went to the observation room.

“He’s telling the truth!” Remi blurted as he opened the door.

“Hold on,” he said. Closing thc door so no one else could hear, he glanced through the one-way glass and saw Luigi and the monk chattering away in Italian while a bored-looking cop stood at the door.

As he turned to her, Remi said, “I don’t think he’s the killer.”

“You believe this bullshit story?” Daniel agreed. “A secret order of monks entrusted to guard a secret they know nothing about? No phones but they know everything that’s happening in the world? A priest who knows how to pick locks? Get real! This guy's either delusional or the most imaginative liar in the world."

"He didn't have a knife. He didn't try to kill me. He didn't even resist arrest. And why come up with a story about a holy order that you can check on? The Vatican will know if it exists or not. Call the Holy See in Rome and ask."

Daniel blinked. She had a point. Remi went on.

"He came all this way to grab the pyxis, and when it was nearly in his grasp, I stopped him. The real killer would have hacked his way right through me. Nothing would have stopped him but a bullet."

Daniel looked uncertainly at the suspect, and then back at her. "We need to hold him. Something about this stinks."

"I agree. Is the museum secure?"

"Don't worry about the museum. There are two cops stationed inside and a patrol car in the area. I made sure of that."

Remi did not look relieved. "Yes, but it's got to be us who catches him. Don't you see?"

Daniel tried to keep his patience. "Yes, I do see. Because you want a crack at the cryptex yourself. Just like the killer does, and by that, I mean the real killer, not numb nuts in there."

Remi looked puzzled. "What does numb nuts mean?"

"Never mind. What do you know about this monastery?"

"Nothing."

"Nothing? The guy says they're sworn to guard the cryptex."

Remi shrugged. "If that was so, then I'd have heard about it."

"So he is lying. Either that, or they're good at keeping secrets."

Remi got on her phone. After a minute she said, "I did find it listed on the Vatican online register. Like he says, it's near Ravenna. There's virtually no information on it that I can see. This isn't uncommon for the more traditional monasteries and nunneries. You'll have to ask the Vatican for more."

"How old is it?"

Remi tapped away at her phone for a while. "The order of St. Adrian of Nicomedia was founded in 1295 by someone named Father George of Constantinople. I can't find anything more about it, or him."

Daniel felt his interest rising.

"You mentioned the cryptex was probably made near the end of the thirteenth century, in either Byzantium or northern Italy. With the

Constantinople connection we have both. Could these guys have made it?"

Remi smiled. "You are an attentive student."

Daniel grinned. "I won't fall asleep in any of your lectures, professor, not while that nutcase is running around. Do you think these monks made it?"

"It's possible. Many medieval monasteries had craft centers. They're mostly known for making illuminated manuscripts, but they made other items too."

"Like beer."

Remi rolled her eyes.

"Medieval monks produced more important products than beer."

"Oh, I disagree. There's no greater work of art than a good glass of beer."

"You don't strike me as a drinker. You're too driven. Too serious."

"I was joking," Daniel said.

"It's hard to tell with Americans. I wouldn't blame you if you did drink. If I had to deal with killings and murder scenes every day, I suspect my consumption of wine would at least double."

Daniel inclined his head. "Alcoholism is actually a big problem in law enforcement. I've steered clear of that. Ever try to do a stakeout while hung over? Not something you want to try more than once. Speaking of stakeouts, we need to get back to the museum."

To his surprise, she shook her head. "He won't break in tonight."

"How can you be so sure?"

"He watches the museum before he breaks in. You said so yourself. He always comes straight for the door he wishes to unlock and moves without hesitation through the museum. That shows he visits the museum during opening hours, and also watches the building at night to find the best place to break in. I suspect he was watching tonight. He might have seen the monk enter the museum, and he certainly would have seen all those flashing lights and wailing sirens when the police showed up to take the monk away. You American police certainly love your drama. He won't try tonight. It's too risky for him."

"But what if he wasn't watching?"

"Then he isn't here yet."

"Or we have the wrong place," Daniel suggested.

Remi looked through the one-way glass at the monk.

“No,” she said softly. “We don’t have the wrong place. Otherwise, this monk wouldn’t be here. Luigi is right, he won’t lie. But that doesn’t mean he will tell us everything he knows. I think the Order of St. Adrian of Nicomedia knows exactly what’s in that pyxis, and I think the killer knows it too.”

Remi stamped her foot in frustration.

The poor academic, finding the real world knows more than she does.

As soon as he thought that, he felt it unworthy. She was different than most. Your typical professor couldn’t have held up under all this strain.

“So he’ll strike tomorrow,” Daniel said, anticipation rising as it always did when he was getting close. This woman had an amazing mind. “We’ll head over to the museum around closing time and stake it out all night.”

“Yes,” Remi said softly. “Yes, I think tomorrow is the day.”

CHAPTER TWENTY THREE

Remi stood in front of the pyxis, staring at its beautiful lines and delicate engravings, and wanting nothing more than to smash open the display case and pry open the top and bottom, looking for hidden compartments.

She had stood there for the better part of an hour, as the late afternoon crowds had swirled around her, staring and staring at every line of the object, hoping to notice a seam or catch. Something, anything to indicate the cryptex was hidden inside.

She could see nothing, of course. If the cryptex had remained inside the box for all these centuries, any secret compartment would be so well hidden that no casual study would ever reveal it.

Now she understood why the Cryptex Killer, as Daniel so overdramatically called him, had broken the objects instead of searched through them. In a burglary, time was of the essence. He needed to get what he wanted and get out.

But he had also twisted that necessity into something entirely unnecessary—the slaying of an innocent human being. He had made as much noise as he could in order to summon the nearest guard like a lamb to the slaughter.

Why? She still didn't understand this. Daniel had said it was probably a part of a ritual that most serial killers had in order to make sense of their senseless actions, to give meaning to meaningless cruelty.

That might very well be true, but she also had to wonder if something deeper was going on. It turned out that despite all her studies, most of cryptex lore had remained hidden to her. She hadn't even suspected that the Order of St. Adrian of Nicomedia even existed until the previous night. What else didn't she know? Could the killer be part of a different order, a more deadly organization? Or maybe that monk hadn't been telling the whole truth, and the killer was a rogue member of the Order of St. Adrian of Nicomedia.

She couldn't say. All she knew was that this pyxis in front of her held a secret so profound that people were willing to devote their lives to it, that an entire sacred order dedicated to its guardianship had survived for centuries. This conspiracy ran far, far deeper than she had ever suspected.

That left her feeling very much alone. She had devoted her entire professional career to this subject, and it turned out she knew far less than she had assumed.

Father Orselli, the captured priest, had clammed up. All he would say was that he was innocent, and the real killer was still out there.

That appeared to be the truth. A search of his hotel room had turned up his passport. Daniel had checked with Customs and Immigration and found he had entered the United States via Hartsfield-Jackson Atlanta International Airport the same day he had tried to break into the High Museum. So unless he had managed to somehow fake all that, Father Orselli was not the killer.

He was still in a jail cell for breaking and entering, though.

Remi felt sorry for him, and furious at Daniel for not letting her speak with him.

A soft tone chimed over the P.A. system.

"The museum will be closing in fifteen minutes. Please make your way to the front exit. Thank you for visiting the High Museum of Art. Have a pleasant evening."

Remi grimaced. She'd have anything but a pleasant evening. She'd be stuck on watch in the museum, agonizingly close to the answer to all her questions and unable to even sneak a peek.

Unless ...

No. There was a security guard in the camera room at all times. He'd raise the alarm if she broke into the display case. Indeed, the case itself was alarmed. She was no burglar who could circumvent electronic alarms and change security camera footage to fool trained guards.

But perhaps there's some way. Tonight, I could probably get the guard to leave, for a bit, saying I'd watch over the cameras so he could take a bathroom break or something. Or better yet, tell him he needed to check on something on the other side of the museum. That would give me a few minutes to run down here and open the case.

But how to disable the alarm? There must be a control panel for that somewhere. I know! I could ask them to double check it, then see where it is. These security guards aren't too bright. I could probably get away with that.

Remi shook herself to banish these insidious thoughts. What was she thinking? Breaking into a display case and destroying an artifact? How could she even entertain the thought? It went against every code of ethics she had ever held dear.

But what about the cryptex? Wasn't it wrong to leave it undiscovered and unstudied?

And it wasn't like she'd smash the pyxis to pieces. She'd try to find the secret compartment without damaging such a beautiful work of art.

Even better, if she could retrieve it and leave the secret compartment open for the killer to see, then he wouldn't break the artifact either.

Unless he flies into a rage. Unless being stopped at the last minute makes him start a killing spree.

You're playing with fire, Remi. You should stay in your archives and classrooms.

But what's the point of those archives and classrooms if I can't advance knowledge?

"All right, folks, the museum is closing. Please make your way to the front exit."

The security guard passed right behind her. Making Remi feel a spike of guilt, even though she hadn't done anything.

Remi glanced around. The security guard was already moving into the next gallery, repeating his announcement. The few people remaining in the temporary exhibition started moving toward to main hall that led downstairs and to the front doors. They moved slowly, taking long last looks at the beautiful works of art around them.

One person did not move at all.

He was a large man, perhaps six-two, with a strong build. His face was stony, impassive, with deep frown lines. He stood remarkably still about five paces away from Remi.

Only his eyes showed life. They practically blazed with emotion, an emotion Remi had trouble reading. What did she see there? Greed? Rage? Ecstasy? A combination of all three emotions and perhaps more?

One thing she could tell for sure—he was staring right at the pyxis.

Remi's soul trembled. Common sense told her this could not be the person she thought it must be. That no one would walk through the museum this boldly during visiting hours. The real killer would be far more subtle.

And yet … who else would look at the cryptex with such emotion?

Remi looked away, consciously trying to get a hold of the swirl of emotions inside her. Fear fought with curiosity, which fought with a strange, twisted sense of camaraderie. She had absolutely no idea what to do.

Run to the nearest security guard, you fool.

She found she couldn't. Instead, she stayed rooted to the spot.

At least look at him, take in more details of his appearance to tell the police.

She adjusted her hair, using that as a cover to angle her head and peek at him out of the corner of her eye.

He still stood there, staring at the pyxis, seemingly unaware that the gallery was emptying out and she was the only one beside him not moving.

The man wore a workman's checkered shirt and jeans. On his feet were heavy boots of the kind construction workers wore. They were probably steel-toed, and one kick from those powerful legs would shatter her bones.

Remi trembled.

She trembled again when she noticed something else about those boots.

That had little bright speckles on them.

What were those? Glitter? That seemed like an odd thing for such a man to have on his boots. Briefly she had a vision of him attending a little girl's birthday party and felt ill.

She glanced over and focused on the boots. Was that gold? It certainly looked like gold.

Remi turned to face the pyxis, her entire body going chill.

Gold. Gold paint. She had read about that in the report about the break in at the Glencairn Museum. Remi had read through all of Daniel's reports, carefully skipping the grisly photos but assiduously examining every other detail.

And one detail thrust out from among all the others to hit her like a bullet between the eyes.

The CSI lab in Pennsylvania had sampled some clay that had been tracked in from the murderer at the Glencairn Museum and had found a little flake of gold paint.

Remi stiffened. She felt the blood pulse in her ears. The pyxis went out of focus. She blinked. Licked her lips. She wasn't sure she was breathing anymore.

Slowly, as if not from her own will, she turned to face the man with the gold paint on his boots.

And found him looking right at her.

Those eyes bored into hers. Remi opened her mouth, trying to speak, but no words came.

His expression subtly changed. The burning heat of intense emotion remained, but it had softened somewhat. It had also changed. The rage had vanished. Now there was a different look in his eyes. The determination remained, but now had been diluted with a certain sense of satisfaction and, as those flaming eyes looked directly into hers, a sense of … collusion?

Remi would not have been surprised if he had winked.

But such a serious-looking man probably never made a gesture like that. And in fact, he did not need to. His eyes expressed enough. It was as if one member of a team cast a knowing look at another.

"You may not have the mind of a killer, but you want the same thing. You are, to be blunt, just as obsessed as he is."

Professor de Villepin's words came back to her and made twice as much sense as they had than when he had first said them.

For she was staring right at the man they had been hunting, and she wasn't raising the alarm.

He had learned things Remi had never suspected, had gotten closer to solving the cryptex than perhaps anyone in eight hundred years.

And even more, he had the ability to get the cryptex and unlock its secrets.

She had to talk with this man.

What am I thinking? He's a killer! Talk with him when he's in a jail cell.

A soft tone chimed over the P.A. system, making Remi jump.

"The museum will be closing in ten minutes. Please make your way to the front exit. Thank you for visiting the High Museum of Art. Have a pleasant evening."

The man gave Remi an almost imperceptible nod.

Remi shook herself, the spell of those eyes broken. Glancing around, she saw she was now in the gallery alone.

Alone with the killer.

She needed to find a guard!

She rushed to the next room, only to find a couple of museum-goers. No guard.

Remi turned and froze. This room was a dead end. She was trapped. The killer was still in the next room. He had seen her, nodded at her. If she went back in there, who knows what he might do to her?

Remi stood behind the doorway, hidden from view of the next room as the two other members of the public innocently wandered around looking at the displays. Her ears strained to hear the sound of smashing plexiglass. No sound came.

He won't do it now, not with people around. He never does. He'll come back tonight to steal it.

Not if I can help it.

She called Daniel. His phone was busy.

Damn it!

What could she do? She couldn't pass by him.

He must have recognized me. Of course, he doesn't know that I'm involved with the investigation. Daniel has managed to keep that fact away from the press. So this man must assume I'm on the trail too, and that I'll meet up with him tonight outside the museum.

Maybe that means he won't hurt me. Maybe he needs me.

I can't let him go. I have to risk passing him.

Summoning up her courage, she stepped back into the room containing the pyxis.

He was gone.

Remi walked at a quick pace out the gallery. She came to a smaller room containing a ticket counter for the temporary exhibitions and a small shop where exhibition catalogs and other mementos were for sale. Other than a member of staff counting out the register, no one else was there.

She hurried out of the room and came to the landing of a staircase curving down to the main floor. The man was not in sight. She hurried halfway down the steps, until she got to a point where she could look out over the front hall.

The last trickle of the crowd was heading out. Remi scanned the people, looking for him.

He was nowhere in sight.

CHAPTER TWENTY FOUR

That evening, as the Chosen One drove into downtown Atlanta from his motel on the outskirts of the city, he felt something he hadn't felt since that horrible summer in Bible Camp.

Joy.

He had gone to the High Museum during visiting hours to case out the layout like he had the previous day. Since he had seen that other man get arrested, the Chosen One knew he had to be on his guard. He had watched as two men who looked like plainclothes policemen had come out of the museum with the intruder.

Out of the museum. They had been lying in wait.

And most likely they would be lying in wait again tonight.

Because Professor Remi Laurent was still with them. She had figured out the pyxis contained something of importance, although even she probably did not know it contained the cryptex itself. Mostly likely she thought it contained another clue.

She would have also figured out that man they had captured was not the man who had broken into the other museums.

Just as he had despaired, thinking she was the enemy, God had set her in his path.

As he came into the temporary exhibition to study the layout a second time, she had been there, staring at the pyxis.

For a couple of minutes, he had stood nearby, watching her, admiring her beauty, and noting the joy and curiosity with which she gazed at the pyxis.

And then she saw him, and God revealed His reward.

Professor Laurent—no, *Remi*—had recognized him. She had looked surprised, afraid, and yet she did not run screaming for a security guard. She did not raise the alarm. As he left the museum, no one pursued.

The Chosen One's prayers for a companion had been answered. Just as he hoped, Remi was working from the inside, pretending to help the police investigation to get closer to the pyxis.

Closer to him.

“Hallelujah! I’m going to have a mother!” Little Peter cheered from the seat next to him.

“That’s right,” the Chosen One said in his own gravelly voice. “And you will soon have brothers and sisters too.”

“Godly brothers and sisters,” Little Peter said. “As pure as my gold paint. My father and mother will protect them. No one will ever make them impure.”

“I will be their guardian,” the Chosen One said. “No one will sully them like that devil in human guise sullied me in Bible Camp.”

“God smiles on you,” Little Peter said.

The Chosen One nodded.

“He’s cleared a path for you,” Little Peter went on. “He’s even shown you a way to sneak into the museum without the cameras seeing.”

“Yes,” the Chosen One said. “They will suspect, of course, and I will not have much time, but woe betide any who get in my way.”

“Their blood will be your redemption,” Little Peter told him.

The Chosen One parked a few blocks from the museum. Like the previous night, he wore his repairman disguise and carried his toolbox.

Inside the toolbox, besides all the necessary tools, he had all the clues, the dodecahedron, and his knife.

As the Chosen One got out of the van, Little Peter, who still sat in the passenger’s seat, said, “Bring me back a mommy, and bring me back the cryptex. If you do that, God will make you pure. You will never feel sullied again.”

The Chosen One gripped his toolbox tight and headed for the museum.

* * *

Remi felt everyone in the room could see right through her.

Especially Daniel.

They sat in the camera room of the High Museum, hours after Remi had seen the killer, and she still hadn’t been able to bring herself to tell anyone about it.

The time for that had long passed. She should have shouted when she had first seen him, run out of the gallery calling for help no matter what the risk. Or she could have made the excuse that she was too scared and then warned the security guards after the killer had left. At the very least she should have told Daniel when she met him half an hour after closing, made up some story about seeing someone staring at the pyxis and only figuring out his identity after the fact.

Now it was far too late. To admit seeing him now would be tantamount to admitting that she had let him slip away. Daniel would have certainly taken her off the case and she would have returned to Georgetown in disgrace, never getting the chance to inspect the cryptex.

Remi finally understood the full meaning of the expression "silence is complicity."

Daniel sat next to the security guard looking at the bank of cameras while a plainclothes police officer stood nearby. Another plainclothes officer and two security guards patrolled the extensive museum buildings. A third plainclothes officer was stationed in front of the locked door to the exhibition at all times. No one paid any attention to her. Even so, she couldn't imagine they couldn't see the guilt and confusion brimming up inside of her.

How could she have let him go? Just so they could see inside the pyxis? He must have all the clues by now, and tonight he'd try to break in, and they could use the clues to unlock the cryptex.

Wait. Was she lumping herself in with that maniac who slit people's throats?

Professor de Villepin is right. I really am obsessed.

No, I am not like him. What I'll do is wait until he breaks in. They'll catch him, and I can get the clues. He probably has them on him. After a lifetime of searching, he won't want to wait another minute to unlock the cryptex. He'll do it right there and then.

When they grab him, I'll unlock the cryptex, myself. I'll use his skills to get me access to the artifact, and then find the secret for myself.

Remi did not feel guilty about using the killer in this fashion. It was a deceitful, underhanded thing to do, but this man killed people. She owed him nothing. He had no moral right to the cryptex.

So no, she did not feel guilty.

But she sure did feel guilty about putting all these people in peril.

Daniel's usual grumbling made her focus on the present.

"What idiot set up these cameras?" he said, waving his hands in the air. "There are blind spots everywhere."

"You get that with most buildings," the security guard said with a shrug. "Cameras cost money and the museum went with a cheap option. At least the entire exterior is covered. Same with the exhibition spaces."

"Yeah, but we ran around blind in the storage area. And there are dozens of blind spots inside the public area too. You don't even have a camera for the east stairs!"

"We do. It's busted."

Daniel groaned.

The security guard gave him an apologetic look. "At least we can see the outside. Anyone comes within one block of the perimeter and we can spot him, just like we spotted that guy last night."

"And then had to chase him around blind," Daniel muttered. He perked up. "Hey! Camera seven. That guy passed by twice already."

Remi peeked over their shoulders as they leaned in to look at the image of a man walking down the sidewalk.

"Looks lost," the security guard said.

"Or faking being lost so he can pass by a few times," Daniel said.

The man stopped, waved, and a car pulled up. He climbed in and the car pulled away.

"I'm going to the coffee machine," the plainclothes officer said. "Anyone want anything?"

Daniel handed him a dollar. "Get me a Three Musketeers from the candy machine."

"All right," the officer said, leaving the camera room.

Everyone else turned back to the bank of cameras.

"What about these two on camera twelve?" the security guard asked, pointing. "The guy is big and burly, like the perp from the other museums."

Remi saw a couple walking down the road, a huge man and a petite woman.

"He wouldn't be with a woman," Daniel said with a shake of his head. "And see how he's twirling his car keys around the forefinger of his left hand? The perp is right-handed. That's not our guy. What about the guy on camera four?"

Remi looked to camera four and swayed in her seat, suddenly lightheaded. A burly man worked on an electrical box near the northeast corner of the museum. While he stood at the very edge of the camera's focus, Remi knew him immediately.

She opened her mouth to speak.

"Don't worry about him," the security guard said. "See that logo? It's the municipal repairs company. They come down here at night all the time."

Doubt made her pause. If the security guard recognized him …

"OK. Now what about those three loitering across the street?"

… no, he only recognized the logo. Remi looked more closely at the figure on camera four. Was it him?

"You mean camera two? One guy looks big. But didn't you say the perp was a loner?"

It was. It had to be,

"Probably. But he could be masking himself in a group. Let's keep an eye—"

Suddenly, the lights cut out.

CHAPTER TWENTY FIVE

Remi was up and running a second later. By memory she ran down a short hallway, hands outstretched until she banged into the staff door. She flung it open and just as quickly shut it behind her.

Now she was in one of the upper galleries. A few small, high windows let a little of the streetlight to filter in, just enough that she didn't knock over any priceless art as she passed.

Still, she couldn't run like she wanted to, only manage a quick walk. She did not dare turn on the flashlight on her phone.

She jumped, suppressed a yelp as the staff door she had passed through banged open a second time, the beams of two flashlights poking into the darkness. Remi ducked behind a large bronze sculpture.

"Where's the emergency generator?" she heard Daniel ask.

"This way."

"Come on, let's move. He's going to try and get inside."

"You don't know that."

"Like hell I don't."

Remi heard their footsteps recede, the light from the flashlights fade, then suddenly get much weaker as they passed a corner. In their hurry to get to the generator, they seemed not to have noticed she wasn't still in the office.

She hurried as fast as she could through another gallery, then down a flight of stairs overlooking the central foyer two floors below. Her shoes echoed thorough that great black space, making her heart race even faster.

An old fear of the dark, forgotten since adolescence, returned.

Steeling herself, she got to the next floor, the one where the temporary exhibition was.

She stopped short. Where had the plainclothesman gone, the one guarding the door?

The sound of footsteps coming up the stairs from the main floor made her hurry back to the opposite gallery and duck behind the doorway.

The footsteps continued, still in the middle distance, then stopped.

"Freeze!" someone shouted.

A loud metallic crash, a groan, and the thud of a body hitting the marble floor. Remi yelped in fright, then clapped her hand on her mouth.

She froze, ears perked. Had the killer heard her?

What am I doing here? I'm going to get myself killed.

Remi glanced at the stairway leading to the next floor. She could run up that way and be out of it. The killer would not chase her into a different floor of the museum when he was so close to his goal.

But she found she couldn't move. Her whole life had been building up to this point. She couldn't run away now.

Unless that psychopath came for her. Then she'd run so fast she'd be back in Paris before sunrise.

She did not hear the sound of approaching footsteps, or—and she dreaded this most of all—him calling her by name. Instead, she heard the faint rasp of metal on metal.

Remi dared a peek. At the locked door to the temporary exhibition gallery, she saw a hulking shadow kneeling. A body lay stretched out on the floor nearby, as well as a toolbox.

That must have been what I heard. The policeman got too close, and the killer knocked him out with his toolbox.

He wouldn't have been hurt if I hadn't frozen up this afternoon.

Guilt washed over her as the killer continued to work on the lock.

Little light came from the high, distant windows, and yet the man seemed to exude an air of confidence, almost as if he worked by feel.

He must have, because a few seconds later there was a click, the man stood, opened the door, and slipped inside, leaving it partially open.

He'll have to pick the lock on the next door. I'll wait here until he does.

She cocked an ear but heard nothing. Where was everyone? How long would it take to get the backup generator on?

A wan light shone within the gift shop leading to the temporary exhibition gallery. Remi stared at it curiously a moment before she figured it out. There were no windows in that room and no emergency exit with its little red light. The killer couldn't work completely blind.

Killer, Remi. He's a killer. Remember that.

That wasn't going to stop her from following him. When the faint sound of the far door opening came to her ears, she tiptoed after him.

Run, one part of her pleaded. *What are you doing? Run!*

I can't. I have to see.

No, she reminded herself. *You have to check on this poor police officer first.*

She crouched over the policeman and to her relief found he was still breathing.

Relief turned to greater fear as she discovered his gun was missing.

Just as she crossed the landing toward the door to the gift shop annex, she heard a distant sound come from downstairs. It had sounded like a thud. She paused, listened. The sound did not repeat.

Then a crash inside the temporary exhibition gallery made her jump.

Crouching low, Remi moved into the gift shop, guided by a light shining from around the half open door at the far end.

With her heart threatening to tear itself out of her chest, Remi angled to the right so she could look through the door while remaining half hidden by a display of books.

He was there. He must have felt pressed for time because he had simply smashed the display case instead of opening it. A flashlight shone in one hand and in the other, a wrench that he used to clear away the hole he had made in the thick Perspex. An open toolbox lay at his feet.

A faint sound behind her made her swing around. She did not see anything, but with the door she had passed through barely open enough for her to have fit, and near darkness beyond that, how would she see anything anyway?

There came another soft, unidentifiable sound. She couldn't tell how far away it was, or even if it was closer than the first sound.

Remi turned back to face the killer, who now had the pyxis in his hands. He opened it up, looking inside. The flashlight lay by the side of the broken display case, illuminating the medieval ivory jar and lid.

He's going to break it!

Remi reached for her pepper spray, only to discover she had left it in her purse back at the camera room.

The killer raised both parts of the pyxis and smashed them against the base of the display case.

"No!" she cried, an instinctive response to seeing a priceless artifact broken.

Remi clamped her hand to her mouth, far too late. The killer whirled around, grabbing the flashlight and beaming it directly at Remi. She held her hand up against the glare.

"Don't be frightened, Remi. I won't hurt you," he said in a hoarse, croaking voice.

She froze, unable to run.

"Come here."

Remi shook her head.

The flashlight left her face and shone on something in the killer's hand. Remi sucked in a long breath.

It was a rectangle of ivory squares a little longer and wider than a wallet. Even at the distance of ten meters and with only a flashlight shining on it, she could see each square had writing.

"Come. The solution is quite simple. On two separate pieces of paper, they wrote the code. Each part of the code is discovered by using these small calipers to measure a certain side or hole of the Gorizia dodecahedron. Then you measure along the cryptex and turn the square the calipers reach."

"I-I thought it would be something like that." Remi's voice came out hushed, hoarse.

"Come."

She didn't move.

"Come. Let's open it together. I swear to God, I won't hurt you."

The way he said it, the emphasis and devotion he put on "God", made her believe him. He would kill to get what he wanted, but he would not kill her.

Her research had helped lead him to this point. She was special to him.

"Come. Let's discover this secret together."

Remi found herself moving forward. The whole scene felt unreal, as if she was another person looking upon herself. She gazed at the cryptex in his hand. As she drew closer, she could see the numbers and Latin letters on the squares.

"It's simple," the killer explained. "I have the list of clues right here. They were hidden in two different slips of parchment. Here's the first. It says, 'The first three squares: shortest, longest, widest hole.' So I take the calipers and measure the shortest side of the dodecahedron."

"Yes, that's what I thought!" Remi said stepping forward.

Then she froze. A glint of metal had made her look down. Inside the toolbox at the killer's feet lay a large knife, like a butcher's knife.

"That's not for you," the killer said in an offhand way.

"W-where's the gun."

He seemed surprised at the question. "The gun? Oh, I threw that away. Sacrifices must be made in the old way. I have no need for guns." He gestured at the cryptex. "Now that I've measured the shortest side, I measure from the left end of the cryptex and find it aligned with the letter D. For "Dios". How appropriate. Relax, Remi. Look at the cryptex, not my toolbox. You are safe with me. I need you. You need me. Whatever this device reveals we will use it together."

Remi trembled. She could not forget that this man was a brutal murderer, and yet she could not run, could not scream for help. The centuries-old ivory device in his hands had hypnotized her.

"I did that only to demonstrate. I've already measured the various sides of the dodecahedron and written them on this paper here. So the longest side is 271 millimeters. I don't know what measurements they used back then. I'm sure you could tell me. There's so much a wise, Godly woman like you can teach me. There will be plenty of time now. So that measurement aligns with the number 3. The trinity. Now the next measurement—"

"Freeze!"

An unfamiliar voice startled them both. A flashlight spot-lit them. Remi felt a sudden surge of guilt.

"Hands up! Step away from the woman. It's all right, professor. You're safe now."

Remi recognized the voice now. It was one of the security guards.

"You! Keep your hands in the air. I said step away."

The killer gently set the cryptex down on the shattered display case next to the calipers and took two steps away from it. He squinted. Remi watched, edging away, as his gaze lowered to focus on the brown pants and dress shoes.

The uniform of a museum security guard.

An unarmed security guard.

A man who was trying to stop a serial killer with nothing more than a bluff.

The killer roared and rushed the guard. Remi saw the blur of a nightstick and heard the thwack of wood on the killer's shoulder.

It didn't even slow him down. He barreled into the security guard and they both fell hard on the floor, the flashlight rolling away. Remi screamed and backed off, unsure what to do.

The two men rolled back and forth on the floor, struggling.

Remi glanced at the cryptex sitting on the display case, just one step away. Just one step and grab it. She could run. No one would even now she had it. It could all be hers …

The killer punched the guard once, twice, then scrambled to his feet and rushed over to the toolbox.

He pulled out the long, sharp knife. It gleamed in the shine of the two flashlights.

The sight of it sparked Remi into action.

"No!"

She jumped between the groaning security guard on the floor and the killer who was stalking toward him.

"Out of the way, Remi. I must make the sacrifice."

"No!" she repeated, stretching out her arms, palms toward him. "You can't kill him."

He took another step forward, getting terrifyingly close. "I must."

"No. God shows mercy. He's given you the cryptex, right?" Remi realized Daniel's theory of a religious maniac was true. Perhaps this was the way to get to him.

"True, but God also requires a sacrifice in return for His gracious favor."

"Haven't you sacrificed enough? Not just the security guards, but your own life. How many years have you spent on this quest?"

The killer slumped a little. "So many."

"Yes, so many years. So many lonely years. Now God is rewarding you."

The killer stood a little straighter and managed a smile. "Yes. You're right. He is rewarding me."

The way he looked at her made Remi's stomach twist, and she came to a sudden, horrible realization.

Her skin crawled.

Licking her dry lips, and clearing her throat so she could speak once more, she tried to keep her voice level as she said,

"Yes. The Lord is rewarding you. With me. Let this man go and you can have me. You won't be alone anymore."

CHAPTER TWENTY SIX

"Let this man go and you can have me. You won't be alone anymore."

Remi's words from the next room spurred Daniel into action.

He had just made it to the annex of the temporary exhibition space, gun leveled and at the ready. That idiot from the camera room was having trouble getting the emergency generator started, so Daniel had given up and set out for here on his own, only to find the officer guarding the exhibition knocked unconscious. He had no idea where the other two cops were. One was on the other side of the museum and would take ages to get here in the dark. The other one seemed to have gotten lost on his way back from the vending machine.

Daniel peeked through the half-open door, careful not to reveal himself. It sounded like the killer had Remi, and he couldn't just leap in there.

What he saw proved he had made the right decision.

From what little he could make out from the two flashlights, both pointing in the wrong direction, a security guard lay half-conscious on the floor. Remi stood with his back to him, and a few steps beyond loomed the killer, knife in hand.

Daniel barely noticed the shattered display case beyond, or the strange ivory device sitting where the pyxis had once been.

"Let him go," Remi said. "We have what we need."

Damn, you got some guts professor. Now I got to figure out how to save your snooty French ass.

In a gravelly voice, the killer said, "You are merciful, and that is the way a woman should be. But this is man's work. A man's Godly work, and you must—"

Daniel pulled out his mini mag lite and threw it across the room. With the killer talking he didn't hear it as it flew through the air, only when it clattered on the far side of the gallery. He spun, brandishing the knife.

No time to lose. Daniel burst into the room, angling to the right to get Remi out of the line of fire. The killer, hearing the new noise, spun to face him and leapt forward.

Daniel fired. The killer spun, blood blossoming from the elbow of his knife arm, the weapon spinning away.

"Freeze!" Daniel ordered. He could not shoot an unarmed man, not even a psycho like this. "Remi, back away!"

Remi backed away.

And so did the killer.

He turned and ran for the doorway leading to the second room of the temporary exhibition space.

"Halt!" Daniel shouted, running after him.

"Get it!" the killer shouted.

Huh?

The killer disappeared into the darkness of the next room and suddenly went silent. Daniel got to the doorway and stopped, eyes peering through the gloom.

"Remi, stay back," he called without turning around. "Help the guard. Do *not* come in here."

Please listen to what I say for once.

The room was almost pitch black, with only the faint light of the killer's flashlight in the other room giving a bit of illumination.

"You're cornered," Daniel shouted into the room. "Come out with your hands up!"

Off to his right, he heard the voice of a young voice wail, "Help me! He's got me all tied up!"

Oh crap, he's taken a kid hostage!

"Stay where you are," Daniel called. "I'm coming for you in a second."

"Please help me. He hurt me."

The voice sounded young. Sounded alone and afraid. Bile rose up in Daniel's throat. He took a few shaky steps toward the sound, then got a hold of himself.

Stay calm. You can't save him if you don't stay calm. The killer might try to get to the kid. He might have another knife.

Daniel edged toward the sound of the child's voice, trying to make out coherent shapes amid the dim shadows of the display cases. In this light, everything looked like a threat. Everything looked like a killer.

"Hurry!" the boy pleaded.

Daniel moved further into the darkness, toward the sound of the voice.

Then whipped around to his left as he heard heavy, labored breathing.

Before he got a chance to see who it was, he got hit with what felt like a Mack truck.

He fell hard on the floor, the heavy weight of the killer pushing the air out of his lungs. His gun fell away into the dark.

For a second, Daniel thought he was a dead man. He could feel the iron-hard muscles and the thick body pressing down on him, but the killer fumbled, unable to strike at him. That gunshot to the elbow not only crippled his right arm. It must have been causing him immense pain.

Daniel decided to add to it.

He slammed his fist into the side of the attacker's head. The man grunted, and Daniel let him have it again.

Daniel twisted his body and managed to knee him in the ribs. He wasn't able to get much strength into it, but he did manage to get out from under him.

Just then that idiot from the camera room figured out how to switch on the emergency generator.

The lights came on, and from the distance of barely two feet, the killer and Daniel blinked in the sudden glare.

The killer recovered first, swinging a vicious left hook with his one good arm.

Daniel brought up his arm to protect himself, but the sheer force alone knocked him on his side.

The killer roared and reached for him. Daniel spotted his gun and scrambled for it, only to get slammed down on the floor.

The killer grabbed him by the collar and hauled him back, Daniel's reaching hand missing the gun by inches.

Daniel shot that arm back and landed an elbow into the guy's gut. He let out an *ooof* and tossed Daniel into a display case. The whole thing toppled over and Daniel with it.

He didn't have time to see if he had destroyed a priceless work of art, because the killer, one arm flopping uselessly at his side, rushed him with death in his eyes.

Daniel leapt up and punched him straight in his shattered elbow.

The killer cried out in agony, staggering back. Daniel dove for his gun, spun to face his antagonist, and found the guy almost on him again, that broad, thick hand reaching for his throat.

Daniel fired, and the bullet went straight through the killer's palm.

The man let out a grunt, staring at the neat hole through his hand and swaying a little from side to side. Daniel clocked him on the side of the head with the butt of his pistol, dropping him.

Despite two bullet wounds and a blow to the head, he was still half conscious as Daniel cuffed him.

Daniel stood, looking around. He didn't see the kid. He did a quick pass around the room and didn't find him.

He returned to the killer and nudged him with his toe.

"Where is he? Where's that little boy I heard?"

A low chuckle rose from the wounded man.

"Tell me, you sicko!" Daniel shouted. His hand went to his gun and half drew it.

"Stop," he heard Remi say.

He looked up. Remi stood at the doorway.

"Don't kill him. We've got him now," she told him.

Daniel took a deep breath, wiped his brow, and returned his gun to its holster.

A pure, childlike voice sang out from over their heads.

"Jesus love me this I know, because the Bible tells me so."

The voice faded away as if floating off into the sky. Daniel stared up at the ceiling, his skin crawling.

The two policemen rushed into the room, guns at the ready.

"Nice of you to make it," Daniel said through labored breaths. "Call the paramedics. We don't want this asshole bleeding out."

"The Lord will smite you!" a child's voice said from the ceiling. Both cops stared up there.

"What was that?" one asked.

"Ventriloquism," Daniel said. "Every serial killer has some weird-ass hobby. That's his."

"Uh, right," one of the officers said. "I'm calling the paramedics right now. Agent Walker, why don't you secure the area while my partner takes care of the perp."

"The area is secure. You two can take it from here, I'm done."

And he was done. Daniel hadn't felt more exhausted in his life.

He slouched into the other room, Remi putting a hand on his shoulder as he passed, to find the other two security guards had made it. One was helping his coworker on the floor while the other stood by the cryptex.

Daniel moved over and stared at it curiously. "So this is it."

The security guard extended a hand. "Please no closer, sir. The intruder broke a priceless artifact. I don't know where this came from, but if it's museum property I'll need the director's authorization to let you handle it."

"It's evidence in a serial murder case, you moron!" Daniel snapped.

Remi came up to him and touched his elbow. "It's all right. Let's go."

"Damn good idea," Daniel grumbled.

"Are you alright? Why did that voice frighten you so much?"

Ravenna. Nantes. Florence.

Daniel opened his mouth to reply …

You've never told anyone but Mom.

And she didn't believe you.

"Nothing," he muttered, looking away.

EPILOGUE

Three days later ...

Daniel sat in Deputy Director Burton's conference room at FBI headquarters. Like his last meeting there, a week previously, he sat at the end of the long conference table facing Burton, the Personnel Director, and Antiquities Division head Keiko Ochiai.

The only person missing was Martin Bradshaw, the Assistant Director for the Behavioral Analysis Unit, Daniel's old boss. Daniel took that to mean he would not be getting his old position back.

There was another change too. The higher ups didn't look like they wanted to eat him for breakfast.

Burton spoke first. "So, Agent Walker, I bet you didn't think transferring you to the Antiquities Division would get you onto a serial killer case." He let out a little laugh.

"I'm just glad we got him, sir."

Noncommittal was generally the best way to go in these meetings.

"And in record time," Burton said. "We're very happy with your performance."

Not happy enough to send me back to the Behavioral Analysis Unit.

Before Daniel could think of a suitably polite answer, Assistant Director Ochiai cut in.

"Although the investigation got off to a shaky start, you got the man in the end, and made a priceless archaeological discovery in the bargain."

Shaky start? You toss me into a new division with no resources against a highly skilled killer who's slashing throats on a nightly basis and you expect me to bag him before you have a chance to drink a second latte?

Once again Daniel managed not to say what was on his mind. Instead, he asked something he had been wondering about.

"I noticed there's been nothing about the cryptex in the press."

Ochiai nodded. "Considering the number of obsessives in the conspiracy theory community who are after this item, we thought it best to keep it out of the papers. Indeed, the Vatican specifically requested it."

"The Vatican?"

"Yes. Through their own channels they heard about Father Orselli's mission to Atlanta. They've asked for him to be released and are in negotiations with the High Museum to obtain the cryptex. The State Department is processing his release right now."

"They're going to release him? He's guilty of breaking and entering."

Burton smiled. "Come on, Agent Walker. A little thing like that means nothing in the bigger scheme of international relations."

"Well, he didn't slash any throats, but why should the Vatican get the cryptex? If the High Museum owned the pyxis, wouldn't they own any object inside it?"

"A legal gray area," Ochiai said. "And the Vatican has deep pockets. The High Museum might get a new wing out of all this."

Daniel leaned forward. "They'd give that much?"

"That's what they're saying," Ochiai replied.

This really is important to them. And I'll bet ten times the value of that new museum wing they won't let Remi or anyone else study the thing. It's going to disappear into a Vatican vault and not be discovered again for another seven hundred years.

The Personnel Director shuffled some papers, cleared his throat.

"That will be all, Agent," he said, and began to stand.

"Sir?" Daniel asked.

He stopped and stared.

"Will I be able to return to BAU now, sir?" Daniel asked, hopeful.

A small smile slowly spread on the Director's face.

"Sorry, Agent," he said. "Not now. Antiquities needs you."

Daniel thought he'd feel crestfallen, but while he felt a momentary disappointment, he was surprised to feel something else taking its place: excitement. This division was more than it seemed, and this last case had been more challenging—and fulfilling—than any routine serial killer case he had tackled in a long time.

As the men filtered out the room, Daniel took a moment, and sat in the empty conference room in the silence, taking it all in. He felt his world spinning, filled with anticipation of the next case.

For some reason, he held up his phone and scrolled through his contacts until he came to Remi's number. He was about to tap it.

But he stopped his thumb midway, letting it hang in the air.

He wanted to talk to her, not about the case, but just to see how she was. He was surprised to realize that he had gotten used to her. That maybe he even missed her.

But he had no reason to call her, he realized.

And slowly, he let his thumb drop and put away his phone.

But maybe, in the near future, he would.

* * *

Remi sat in her office long after the last lecture at Georgetown had finished, cursing the creators of the cryptex.

When they had dragged the killer out of the exhibition area, everyone had followed, including the museum security guard. Despite dutifully standing by the cryptex as the paramedics patched up the murderer and hauled him away with the policemen as escort, he couldn't resist the temptation to follow and stare.

He was only gone a minute, just to the head of the stairs.

A minute was all Remi had needed.

She had followed the instructions and opened the cryptex, its brilliantly crafted system of connected ivory cubes opening up smoothly with the correct code.

Engraved on the interior was a map incised into the ivory surface. It showed a little town carved in minute detail, and a river flowing alongside, and to one side an angling row of hills or mountains.

Across the river from the town and a little downstream or upstream, was an X.

In the lower righthand corner was the floorplan of a church. Halfway down the nave was another X.

Remi had taken several photos with her phone and hurriedly closed the cryptex and put it back seconds before the guard returned.

Now she was staring at the thing, bemoaning her luck.

All this trouble to finally get the cryptex open, only to be face with a map that map was impossible to read!

She had the image blown up on her computer screen and had stared at it so long she could have drawn it from memory. She knew every line, every symbol, even dimension of every shape.

And yet it still meant nothing to her.

Since she had left Atlanta, she had spent virtually every waking hour on the problem, trying to correlate the map in the cryptex to modern topography.

So far, she hadn't been able to come up with a match. One problem was that the map was of a relatively small scale, making the search more difficult. Whoever created the cryptex assumed the reader would already know the region. They'd know what town that was, and what river, and that range of hills or mountains, so why put any labels on them?

She felt like digging up the artist and slapping him. Slapping a skull was probably illegal, though.

She had searched in northern Italy, slowly scrolling through Google Maps at its highest resolution. After a couple days of that, she had switched to southern Italy, with an equal lack of luck. Now she was searching France.

If that didn't work, she'd expand to Germany, England, and then God knows where.

It didn't help that the map was seven hundred years old. The river might have changed it course. The town might have become a city. Or vanished. The church depicted in the lower righthand corner may not even exist anymore.

Ugh.

Remi leaned back, rubbing her bloodshot eyes. She had been overly optimistic when she thought that tracking down a serial killer and opening the cryptex would be the end of her investigations. It looked like they were just beginning.

Deciding to take a break, Remi pulled out her phone. She wanted to call Daniel and tell him she'd snuck a few photos of the inside of the cryptex. He'd be almost as fascinated as she was, and the way he liked to bend the rules he would be sure to wink at what she had done.

She hadn't stolen anything, after all. Knowledge should be for everyone.

But no, he was probably busy chasing some new murderer. She had no reason to call him. Still, she wanted to. Even for no reason. And that surprised her.

Reluctantly, she put her phone away.

She had a feeling that, somehow, she'd be seeing him again soon.

And in the meantime, she had a map to solve.

NOW AVAILABLE!

<u>THE MURDER CODE</u>
(A Remi Laurent FBI Suspense Thriller—Book 2)

THE MURDER CODE (A Remi Laurent FBI Suspense Thriller) is book #2 in a new series by mystery and suspense author Ava Strong, which begins with THE DEATH CODE (Book #1).

FBI Special Agent Daniel Walker, 40, known for his ability to hunt killers, his street-smarts, and his disobedience, is singled out from the Behavioral Analysis Unit and assigned to the FBI's new Antiquities unit. The unit, formed to hunt down priceless relics in the global world of antiquities, has no idea how to enter the mind of a murderer.

Remi Laurent, 34, brilliant history professor at Georgetown, is the world's leading expert in obscure historic artifacts. Shocked when the FBI asks for her help to find a killer, she finds herself reluctantly partnered with this rude American FBI agent. Special Agent Walker and Remi Laurent are an unlikely duo, with his ability to enter killers' minds and her unparalleled scholarship, the only thing they have in common, their determination to decode the clues and stop a killer.

A priceless, historic painting is stolen from a museum in Washington, D.C., and a dead body is found along with it. When the trail leads back to Paris and demands a historian's expertise, FBI Special Agent Walker realizes he has no choice but to ask Remi Laurent for her help again. Together, they need to travel to the Louvre, visit the scene of the first murder, decode the message in the stolen paintings, and stop the killer before he strikes again.

A global manhunt ensues in a race against time, as Remi races to understand the clues, and quickly learns that this killer is more diabolical than anything she could have ever imagined.

An unputdownable crime thriller featuring an unlikely partnership between a jaded FBI agent and a brilliant historian, the REMI LAURENT series is a riveting mystery, grounded in history, and packed with suspense and revelations that will leave you continuously in shock, and flipping pages late into the night.

Book #3 in the series—THE MALICE CODE—is now also available.

Ava Strong

Debut author Ava Strong is author of the REMI LAURENT mystery series, comprising three books (and counting); of the ILSE BECK mystery series, comprising four books (and counting); and of the STELLA FALL psychological suspense thriller series, comprising three books (and counting).

An avid reader and lifelong fan of the mystery and thriller genres, Ava loves to hear from you, so please feel free to visit http://www.avastrongauthor.com to learn more and stay in touch.

BOOKS BY AVA STRONG

REMI LAURENT FBI SUSPENSE THRILLER
THE DEATH CODE (Book #1)
THE MURDER CODE (Book #2)
THE MALICE CODE (Book #3)

ILSE BECK FBI SUSPENSE THRILLER
NOT LIKE US (Book #1)
NOT LIKE HE SEEMED (Book #2)
NOT LIKE YESTERDAY (Book #3)
NOT LIKE THIS (Book #4)

STELLA FALL PSYCHOLOGICAL SUSPENSE THRILLER
HIS OTHER WIFE (Book #1)
HIS OTHER LIE (Book #2)
HIS OTHER SECRET (Book #3)

www.ingramcontent.com/pod-product-compliance
Lightning Source LLC
Chambersburg PA
CBHW030617310726
48979CB00003B/757
9781094392837